S0-AJC-457

DEVIL'S RACE

A LIPPINCOTT PAGE-TURNER

DEVIL'S RACE

AVI

J. B. LIPPINCOTT   NEW YORK

DEVIL'S RACE
Copyright © 1984 by Avi
All rights reserved. No part of this book may be
used or reproduced in any manner whatsoever without
written permission except in the case of brief quotations
embodied in critical articles and reviews. Printed in
the United States of America. For information address
J.B. Lippincott Junior Books, 10 East 53rd Street,
New York, N.Y. 10022. Published simultaneously in
Canada by Fitzhenry & Whiteside Limited, Toronto.
Designed by Joyce Hopkins
1   2   3   4   5   6   7   8   9   10
FIRST EDITION

Library of Congress Cataloging in Publication Data
Avi, 1937—
    Devil's race.

    "A Lippincott page-turner."
    Summary: Sixteen-year-old John Proud is tormented
by the ghost of an evil ancestor, with his own name
and his own face, who was hanged in 1854 for being a
demon.
    [1. Ghosts—Fiction.   2. Devil—Fiction]   I. Title.
PZ7.A953De 1984   [Fic]   84-47636
ISBN 0-397-32094-9
ISBN 0-397-32095-7 (lib. bdg.)

For Lucia

DEVIL'S
RACE

PART ONE

I

I sat alone at the far back of the dim classroom, waiting. At the other end of the room my history teacher silently marked papers. Between us, nothing but rows of empty seats and empty desks. Outside, a thin, dreary rain seeped down. Now and again, thunder echoed faintly like sounds of a remembered battle.

Three times she had called on me, three times I had not even heard. The fourth time she had asked me to stay after school.

I was sixteen, tall, lanky, with a round, almost baby face and a pug of a nose. Mr. Average Nice

Guy. When the girls took a poll, there I was, "Best Boy Pal."

After half an hour the teacher put aside her pen. "John Proud," she said softly, "what is the matter?"

She caught me off guard. I had expected a lecture. Instead, she had asked me the one thing I had been asking myself and could not answer: What was the matter?

"Tired," I offered.

"Not enough sleep?"

In fact I had been sleeping more than usual. "Plenty," I replied.

"Look where you are," she said. "You never used to sit in the back of the room. It's not like you. Has something happened at home?"

"No."

"Some personal problem. A girl friend? Parents?" I shook my head.

"But John," she persisted, "I'm not the only one who's noticed."

I looked down at my hands. Things had been going along fine. Easy. Uncomplicated. The way it had always been. Then, about two weeks ago, it had begun to change. That is, I had changed. I didn't know how or why.

"John," said the teacher, "your grades are good. But something, I just sense it, has happened.

4

"Well," she said to my silence, "if you do want to talk about it, I'm here. I hate to see you acting so troubled. Tell me, during class, what were you thinking about?"

"I . . . I was wondering what's going to happen next."

"Next?"

"Yes."

"What do you mean?"

"I don't know."

"Do you *want* something to happen?"

I considered the question. "Sometimes yes," I answered, "sometimes no."

She sat back; then, with a slight shrug, she changed the subject. "How are you coming along with the family history assignment?"

That assignment. It had been my idea that we trace our families back as far as we could.

"How's it going?" she asked. "You've had two weeks to work on it."

"There," I thought. "It's *there*." Whatever was happening to me had begun with that assignment. It was no problem at first. When I asked my parents for help, they were okay about it. But the further I went back, the vaguer they became.

What was back there? Did I want to know, or not?

"See," said the teacher, "you've drifted off again.

That same look. What were you just thinking about?"

"Nothing," I said.

She sighed. "Well, John," she said, giving up, "better scoot. I'll see you in class."

"Thank you," I said, and left, my mind no longer with her. There was someone who could tell me all I needed to know about my family. Uncle Dave. It was he who had first suggested I look at my family tree those two weeks ago. He had given me the idea.

I'd go back to him.

2

"You sure you *want* to know?" Uncle Dave asked me. We were sitting in his shabby two-room Philadelphia apartment with the pale-green walls and the smell of things old and unwanted.

"Why wouldn't I?"

"I can think of a few reasons."

"Like what?"

Instead of answering, he gave me a look as if he were searching inside me, making me uncomfortable. Then he pulled out scrapbooks and shoe boxes full of old photos and folders of newspaper clippings.

"Your family history," he said, with a sweep of his hand over the dusty pile.

I looked at him, wondering. Uncle Dave had been around as long as I could remember. My father's much older brother, he had a reputation for being strange. In his mid seventies, he was thin, scraggly, with a slack-skinned neck spiked with nibs of white hair. His face was pale, his hands long, thin, blue veined.

He leaned forward on the swaybacked couch, pointing at the paper piles. Why had he saved all that stuff?

He cocked an eye at me. "You really want to know about John Proud, don't you?"

I felt a stir in the air, as if a door had opened.

"Me?" I said, puzzled. After all, that was *my* name, John Proud.

"Never heard of him?"

I shook my head.

He sat back and paused a moment. "Your great-great-great-great-grandfather, John Proud, was hanged in the year 1854."

"Why?"

"He was a demon."

I stared at him.

He gave me a sly gaze in return. "You don't believe me, do you?"

7

"I don't know," I answered uneasily.

From the inside of an old brown envelope he pulled a bit of brittle newspaper. Gingerly, he handed it over. I took it and looked at him. He nodded. I read.

JOHN PROUD HANGED
Confesses Openly to Being a Demon
Throng Witnesses Grim Event

Lebanon, Penna. On the 3rd of September, John Proud, condemned man, was hanged to death before the County Jail. Just before his death he asked to speak a few words and was given permission. In so doing, he poured forth in a venomous, vulgar tongue his true nature, to wit, that he was in truth a demon, and proud of that un-natural fact. Moreover, he swore that though they might hang him, he would never leave in peace, but would return in time to complete his business. The crowd, silenced by this grim visage of evil, waited patiently until John Proud was pronounced dead and no longer of this world.

"What's *visage*?" I asked. I felt even more uneasy, almost sick.

"His face."

"What did it look like?"

"I had a picture of him once," he said as he flipped through the papers. "Lost it, I guess. But he looked, well, like you."

"You're making this up."

8

"I've seen his grave."

"When?"

He hesitated. "Some time ago."

"Where?"

"Out toward Harrisburg. Place called St. Anthony's Wilderness."

"Never heard of it."

"We've got relations near there," Uncle Dave said. "Ever meet Nora Fenton? Third cousin."

I studied him, wondering what he was getting at.

"If you want to go," he continued, "I'll take you. Back and forth over a weekend. I mean, you *are* named after him. Must be a reason."

"No way." I closed my eyes and sat there. I really *did* want to see it, but where that wanting was from I didn't know.

"Well?" he asked.

To my surprise, I heard myself say, "Okay."

Uncle Dave sat back and grinned, satisfied.

3

From Philadelphia we went north on Route 76, moved through the interchange, took the Northeast

Extension, then turned west on Interstate 78. I sat straight in my seat watching the dull landscape slip by. Travel wasn't my thing. I liked staying home. Since we had started I hadn't talked much. But then Uncle Dave said, "They never told you about him?"

I knew he was talking about John Proud. "No," I said.

"Not even your father?"

I shook my head.

"Even though you've got the same name?"

"John was my mother's father's name. That's why I have it."

"Think so?"

"That's what she said."

"Sure?"

I shrugged.

He gave me a sour look. "Ever notice," he said, "the more school kids get these days, the fewer words they use? What am I supposed to do, *guess* what's in your head?"

"Nothing's in my head."

He snorted. "You see, John Proud is a family secret," he said. "Not strictly nice. You hand in that history paper yet?"

"Yes."

"I bet you didn't put him in."

10

I didn't answer.

"Didn't think you would," he said.

I turned away. "I asked my folks about your John Proud," I said. "They think it's just a story."

"My kid brother's a good guy. So's your ma. Smart. Educated, too educated. They have an answer for everything. You think there's an answer for everything?"

"I hope so."

"Once," he went on, "somebody told me: If you have all the answers, you didn't ask the right questions. And if all you have are questions, you haven't listened to the answers."

"But a demon . . ." I protested vaguely.

"Just a word," he snapped.

"For what?"

"Evil."

There was a slight, queer shift in my stomach.

"Word *evil* makes you squirm, does it?"

Suddenly I felt an enormous urge to tell him to shut up, to turn the car around, to head back.

"Everybody has evil in them," I heard him say. "You too."

I shook my head hard. I resented his saying a thing like that about me. "Not me," I murmured.

"All the answers, huh?" he said with a smirk,

11

pressing his foot to the gas pedal. The car crept over the speed limit. I clenched my hands tightly and kept my eyes on the road.

I felt like telling him to drop dead.

4

Lickdale was hardly a town. By the time you knew you were in it, you weren't. There was a grocery store, a post office, an Exxon garage, an Agway Farm Supply Depot. Beyond that there were only private homes, not more than thirty.

Each of the houses, surrounded by a neat yard, seemed to be painted a shade of white. It was late May, but a lot of the yards had piles of wood.

"I haven't seen these people for a good many years," said Uncle Dave as we moved slowly, trying to pick out the right house. "Nora married this local fella, Tom Fenton. Don't recollect what Tom does. Couple of kids, I think."

"How far is it to the cemetery?" I asked.

"Ten miles, maybe."

"And how come it's called St. Anthony's Wilderness?"

He looked around, his eyes blank. "Don't know. Ask them. All I know is that it's the largest forest tract in the area. There's the house." He brought the car to a stop and pointed.

It was a simple frame house, white with green shutters. Flower boxes. A low cyclone fence around the yard.

Uncle Dave pulled into the driveway behind a Chevy van. "On your manners, kid."

As we climbed out, the front door of the house opened and a woman rushed out. "David?" she called.

She was wearing a loose orange shirt and white slacks. Not heavy, but she wasn't slick thin either. Her light-colored hair was on the messy side and the look she had was pure welcome.

"It's me all right, Nora," said Uncle Dave.

Nora—she was younger than I'd thought she'd be—came right over and gave Uncle Dave a bear hug. Then she held him at arm's length and looked him over. "Shame on you for keeping away so long!" She was scolding, but there was only affection in her voice. "Been too darn long."

She looked over to me. "This John?" she asked.

"Himself," said Uncle Dave.

She came up to me, took my hands, gave me a smile and, to my surprise, a hug and a kiss. "The image of your father," she said.

"Come on in," she called, leading the way. "Hungry?"

"I can always use coffee," said Uncle Dave, "and the kid eats to keep his hopes up."

Nora laughed as she led us in. The house was compact, bright, and cheerful, comfortable if not particularly neat.

I set our overnight bags in an alcove by the door, an area piled with parkas, boots, and sports stuff. I noticed skis, a backpack, baseball equipment, and a couple of tennis rackets.

As Nora fussed over coffee, Uncle Dave sat at the kitchen table. For me she poured a big glass of milk, then set out a huge wedge of chocolate cake. Right off the two of them jumped into family talk, who was doing what, where, with whom. Every once in a while Nora would exclaim, "I wish I were more in touch" or "I'm so glad you came."

I listened politely.

After a time she peppered me with questions about my family. I gave the best answers I could.

"Where's Tom?" asked Uncle Dave when that was done.

"He got called out," Nora explained. "He's a line repairman for the phone company, and some cable went down over by Lebanon. They call all hours, at the worst times. More than usual lately. All kinds of crazy things going around."

I looked up. She didn't say more.

"And your kids?" asked Uncle Dave.

"Fine! Martin has Boy Scouts this afternoon. He's really into that. He'll be going to Scout camp this summer. And Ann's working at the Agway. Can you believe it, David, tenth grade, and she's already putting good money aside for college. She's a honey. She'll be here soon.

"But you still haven't told me why you've come," she rushed on. "Just called out of nowhere and said you wanted to visit. Not to see us, I bet."

"Sure it was," teased Uncle Dave.

"Don't con me," said Nora, appealing to me. "Never does tell the whole truth, does he?"

"Really want to know why we've come?" Uncle Dave asked.

"Long as it's legal."

"John here," said Uncle Dave, "had a school thing about family. His father didn't know fiddlesticks about the Prouds. So I told him. Naturally, I told him about—"

15

"You didn't!" Nora said, cutting him off. Her smile had vanished.

"Sure, John Proud. Same name, right?"

"Oh, David."

"Family, isn't it . . . flesh and blood?"

"You really named after him?" she asked me.

"My mother's father," I said.

"That's what he says," teased Uncle Dave. "Thought I'd show him the grave."

Nora folded her arms. "Most people don't know," she said. "I wouldn't go out of *my* way to show anyone, or tell them either."

From a distance I heard a series of deep thumps, like the echo of a bass drum.

"What's that?" I asked.

"What?" said Nora, her mind elsewhere. The series of thumps came again.

"That sound."

"Oh, that," she said, relaxing. "On the other side of St. Anthony's is the Fort Indiantown Gap Military Reservation. During spring and summer the National Guard come up for practice, shooting off their guns. Just playacting. I don't even hear it anymore."

I listened. It sounded real to me.

"Kids do like to sneak in there and pick up shell casings. That part isn't fooling; it can be dangerous. They use live ammunition."

16

"The kids know?" said Uncle Dave.

"About the guns?"

"About John Proud."

Nora drew a breath. "Martin's too young, though good Lord, the things he watches on TV. Do you know what they call the local school team? The Demons. But no," she said, "I've never told him."

"And your girl?"

"Ann? She knows." Nora shook her head, then looked at me. "Do you really *want* to know?"

I nodded slightly, blushing.

"Here I was," she said, "hoping you guys were just paying us a friendly visit. Instead, it's that . . . thing." She got up and put on a light sweater.

"Did David tell you what John Proud *did*?" she asked me.

I shook my head.

"How come?" she asked her cousin.

"Thought it'd be more fun to learn it here," teased Uncle Dave.

"Fun!" cried Nora. She turned to me. "Your namesake liked to hurt people. He would win their trust, then betray them. Torment them, destroy them. Murder them, in fact. No one could have been crueler. He used people in the worst possible way."

All of a sudden I felt anger toward her. It came out of nowhere.

17

5

That anger, quick as it came, caught me by surprise.
I tried to push it away. The next moment a kid burst
into the room. It was Martin, Nora's boy, in his
Scout uniform.

"Hey, Mom," he called, "you'll never guess what
happened. . . ." Then he saw Uncle Dave and me.
Quick as anything, he made the switch to company
manners. "Oh, hi," he said.

"Martin," said Nora, "this is Cousin David. And
this is another of your cousins, John."

Though it was clear he had something important
to tell his mother, the kid was well trained. He came
right over and held out a hand to Uncle Dave.
"Pleased to see you," he said. Then he turned and
gave me a careful looking over.

He was, I figured, twelve, something on the short
side, with bright, smooth cheeks, a downy look. Not
busted out of being a kid yet.

After a moment's hesitation, he held out a hand
to me. "Nice to meet you," he said.

"Want some milk and cake?" asked Nora.

"Sure," he said, and slid around the table.

"John's from the Philadelphia area," Nora explained. "Part of my side of the family, the Prouds."

"Hello!"

I swung around and there was Ann, Nora's daughter. She might have passed for one of those billboard ads for the drink-milk campaigns—she was that kind of pretty. Shorter than me, she was bright-eyed, looking good in a plum-colored running suit. Her shoulder-length hair, lighter than her mother's, was pulled into a ponytail. She took me by surprise.

After the introductions the talk went on from this to that, between Uncle Dave and Nora. Then Nora noticed the clock and announced she'd better get dinner going, and would Martin or Ann take me for a look around town? Martin said, "Mom, I have to tell you what happened on our hike."

"Ann?" her mother said, head cocked to say more than she spoke.

"Want to look around?" Ann asked me.

"Sure," I said, trying to sound very casual.

"Probably not much that would interest you around here," she said as we stood outside, both feeling awkward. "Where do you live?"

"Not far from Philly."

"Get there a lot?"

"Not much. Too big and dirty."

"Is it wild the way some people say?"

"Wouldn't know," I said with a smile.

She took a half turn and waved her arm to include the whole of Lickdale. "Not Sin City," she said, "but I like it. Come on. I'll give you the slow five-minute tour."

As we walked we talked, or rather asked each other questions: schools, plans for college, family, a general inventory. She had an easy, direct, relaxed way. I liked her.

Only as we started back did she ask, "How come you came? Not to see us, was it?"

I wasn't sure what to tell her.

"Well, see, my name is John . . . and John Proud . . . was the oldest family member, and . . ."

She came to a halt. "You're named after *him*?" She looked at me curiously. "Is *that* why you came?"

"Well, *I'm* not named after him, but Uncle Dave wanted to show me where he's buried."

"In the Wilderness," she said. Even as she spoke there was some of that distant, thumping racket as military guns went off. "I've been there," she said. "I go backpacking and hiking in that area a lot. The Appalachian Trail is close by. The cemetery, the one you want, is near Rausch Gap, where the old town is."

"Didn't know there was a town."

"Nothing but ruins."

"A ghost town?"

"Hardly. My father going to take you?"

"I think Uncle Dave knows the way."

"It's a hike. Is he up to it?"

I shrugged, asking, "What's the grave like?"

She turned away. "I only saw it once, and not for long."

"How come?"

"I promised myself I'd never go back," she said. "And I haven't." She turned to look at me. "And I won't."

6

It wasn't until we sat down for dinner, about seven o'clock, that I got to meet Tom, Ann's father. He was a huge guy, maybe six two, with great wide shoulders and big hands. He had a shock of blond hair, blue eyes, and a broad smile that chopped white through a bushy beard. The guy was marked "woodsy," from his boots up.

"Oh, Lord," he said, as he sat down after hugging his wife. "This isn't what weekends are for."

"Big mess?" asked Nora, handing him a can of cold beer.

21

He popped the can. "I don't know. First a car ran down a pole south of Lebanon. The guy claimed the car just took off on its own. Lucky he wasn't killed. Then there were some weird cable problems up north." He rubbed his knees. "Been up on poles all day. Too much of this stuff lately. Someone's making bad equipment, or something . . ."

That something held him a moment. "Anyway, it's nice seeing you guys."

"David and John mean to go up to Rausch Gap to look at the old cemetery in the morning," Nora told him.

"It's not my family tree," said Tom with a wink. Then, more seriously, he considered Uncle Dave. "It's a hike," he warned. "Ann, what do you figure it?"

"Four miles in. Four out," she said.

"Well," said Tom, "it's perfectly level."

Nora looked at her husband across the table. "Maybe you should take them. . . ."

Tom gazed back. There was some silent communication. "Well, sure, I'd like that," he said. "Unless I get called out again."

"I don't want to take your time," said Uncle Dave.

Tom held up a big hand. "Nothing to worry about. I'd really enjoy the hike. Haven't been up there for too long. Ann knows those trails better than I do. You coming?" he asked her.

"I've got a lot of homework to do," she answered quickly.

"Well, get it done. Martin?" Tom asked.

"Little League practice," the kid returned.

Tom let out a little sigh. "Nora?"

She shook her head. "Can't" was all she said.

After dinner Ann washed dishes. I dried. Martin put away.

"Boy," said Martin after a while, "I wouldn't go up there."

"Scaredy-cat?" his sister teased.

"Our Scout leader, Mr. Moot, took us up around there today to see some bird nesting grounds. Everywhere we went they were busted up."

"Raccoons," said Ann.

Martin shook his head. "That's what Mr. Moot said at first. But after the third time, he said it must be vandals, and that it had just been done. He didn't want us to mess with any delinquent teenagers. So we came back and just played ball."

"You just chickened out," said Ann.

"Look who's talking," Martin shot back. "She went camping with her friend Sue. They were going on the Appalachian Trail for six days. They came back in three."

"Sue got sick."

"Oh, sure, sure."

She flicked some soap bubbles at him. "I've been out four days, alone. How many nights have you?"

"Mom says I'm too young."

The argument ended.

After dishes Ann and I went out front and sat on the steps. In her hand she held a tin tube with a bunch of holes in it.

"What's that?" I asked.

"Penny whistle," she said, putting it to her mouth and trying a few notes. "Perfect when you're out in the woods." She gave some more toots. Then we started talking again, agreeing about most things too. Finally, as if there was no need to say more, we lapsed into silence. The night seemed to be full of squeaks, grunts, and general racket.

"What's all the noise?" I asked.

"Night sounds," she said. "Frogs, insects, owls." One by one she told me which was which.

"You know your stuff, don't you?" I said, impressed.

"The Wilderness being so close, we sort of live with it."

"But you don't want to visit the cemetery. How come?"

"You'll see."

Out toward the west there were flashes, like

heat lightning. Then a series of booming noises.

"What's that?"

"Night gunnery practice," she said, as if it was the most natural thing in the world.

After a moment I said, "You going to get your homework done?"

"No offense," she said. "I just don't want to go there. Once was enough." She put the penny whistle to her mouth and began to play.

It was a soft, floating melody, making me think of a bird gliding in and out of moonlight and shadow.

It held me, that music. Her eyes found mine on her, and by the yellow house light I saw that she liked me, really liked me. Well, I liked her too.

7

By eight o'clock the next morning we were sitting around the breakfast table. It was bright, clear, already warm. Nora was there. So was Tom, ready to go. Ann, sleepy and in a white bathrobe to make clear her intention of *not* going, joined us. Martin was watching a TV show in the living room.

There wasn't much talk. Then the phone rang.

Nora answered. "Just a minute," she said, then held the phone out to Tom. "It's your supervisor."

"Oh, Lord," said Tom. He heaved himself up and took the phone.

We all watched.

"Problems," he announced when he hung up. "A big line came down on the other side of Indian Gap. I have to go."

"You went yesterday," protested Nora.

"And I have to go today."

"I can't go with you," Nora said to us quickly. "I promised to help Martin's Little League."

"We can find it ourselves," said Uncle Dave.

"Ann . . . ?" began Nora.

Ann guessed what was coming. Right off she said, "Ma, I've got tons of homework . . ." But the way she said it I knew it wasn't going to stick.

"Come on, sport," her father said. "It'd be better." He nodded toward Uncle Dave.

Ann gave me a look as if it was something *I'd* done. She said, "I'll get ready," and went to her room.

Three quarters of an hour later the three of us— with Ann behind the wheel—were in the Fentons' van. The lunch Nora had packed was stuffed into a lightweight day pack. I was given a two-quart canteen to sling over my neck.

I found myself excited to be finally getting to the place. But Uncle Dave, I noticed, was quieter than usual. As for Ann, she was there, but she wasn't looking happy about it.

"Have a good time," said Nora. "Ann, hon, drive carefully."

"Ma, we'll get there!"

She backed the van out neatly, swung around, and pulled out into the road.

Two miles after leaving Lickdale we were into the hills, the road getting steeper the farther we went. On all sides, millions of trees crowded in like an advancing army.

No one talked. I kept stealing glances at Ann, hoping she would loosen up. When she didn't, I began to think that look she had given me the night before was only something imagined.

"What's that Appalachian Trail you talked about?" I asked, talking to fill the silence.

"It's a wilderness hiking trail about two thousand miles long. Goes from Georgia to Maine."

"And people *walk* it?"

"Not mobs. And mostly not the whole length. But more than you might think. I've met them. Over by Yellow Spring station—"

"What's that?"

"Another of the Wilderness's abandoned towns. Old one. There's a mailbox there. People hiking the Trail leave messages for each other. Not far from Devil's Race."

I looked at her. "Devil's Race?"

"That's what it's called. It's a creek."

"Near where we're going?"

She shook her head. "About five miles farther on."

"What's the most you've ever hiked?"

"In a day?"

"Yeah."

"Seventeen miles," she said.

In all that talk she kept her eyes dead front. I decided I was pushing too much, so I just watched what we passed. Houses had disappeared. The hills were higher, the forest thicker. It wasn't long before we passed a big wooden sign with incised letters reading:

PENNSYLVANIA GAME LANDS
ST. ANTHONY'S WILDERNESS

"Who's St. Anthony?" I asked.

"Supposed to be a finder of lost things and a helper against diabolic possession," Ann said.

"What's he got to do with this place?"

She shrugged. "No one knows for sure. It's just what it's called."

I glanced back at Uncle Dave. He was staring out the window. I wasn't even sure he had heard.

Ann took the van up a long, extra-steep hill where the drop off the roadside was sheer. Beyond, the foliage was bright green, new stuff, with darker patches of pine. We were the only ones going in.

The van made it to the top of the hill, then swung off the road. We were no longer on the regular road, but on a long, wide stretch that was mostly gravel.

Close to a low, swinging gate, Ann brought us to a stop. "Trail head," she announced, setting the parking brake. The air felt fresh, sharper than in Lickdale. Ours was the only car there.

We got out, stretched, locked the van doors.

"Thieves?" I asked.

"You never know."

The gate was a big counterbalanced affair, thirty feet long, not locked, just closed. Off to one side was a bunch of signs, listing rules for the area, like "No unauthorized motor vehicles. No gathering wood for fires." I didn't bother to read all of them.

Ann and I climbed the low gate. Uncle Dave went around. On the other side the road ran straight and level as a yardstick. You could almost see the railroad that used to be there, slicing through the woods.

"John Proud, here we come!" called Uncle Dave suddenly. It was as if he were giving a challenge, or a warning. Without waiting, he set off at a smart pace.

I looked at Ann, wishing she would ease up. But all she said was "We better go," and we followed Uncle Dave. From somewhere, those military cannons beat upon the air.

8

I had a nagging feeling that we were going *into* something, something hard. I tried to push it away. It kept coming back.

At one point, when Uncle Dave was still ahead and Ann and I were walking at our own pace, Ann asked, "How you doing?"

"Okay," I said, glad that she had decided to notice me again.

"You look nervous."

"I do?"

She nodded yes.

Suddenly I said, "What's this all about?"

"When you take this trail," she said, "it's like marching back into history."

"A time machine?"

"Sort of. Everything seems simpler, basic."

I said nothing.

"Want to go back?" she asked.

"No," I answered, surprised she had even asked.

"Okay," she said with a sudden smile that made me feel close to her again, "I might as well enjoy it."

"Think I need to stop a bit," announced Uncle Dave. He was sitting down on a roadside log. We stopped too.

Soon as we did, Ann swung off her pack. "How about some water?" she said to me.

I took off the canteen, unscrewed the top, and handed it to Uncle Dave. He took a swig, then passed it on to Ann. Then me. Meanwhile, from her pack, Ann pulled out a bag of what looked like a mix of candies, nuts, and raisins.

"GORP," she announced.

"What?"

"Good Old Raisins and Peanuts. Quick-energy food."

I took a handful and popped bits into my mouth. Uncle Dave did the same, but slower.

"How you doing?" I asked Uncle Dave.

"Don't worry," he said irritably. "I'm still here."

Ann was watching Uncle Dave carefully. The next moment, without saying a word, she jumped into the woods. Uncle Dave and I just waited. In moments she returned with a big stick in her hand. "Walking stick," she said, offering it to Uncle Dave.

"Fancy name for a cane," he said, but he took it anyway.

In a few moments we started off again, Uncle Dave using the stick. I kept my distance.

We hit the first of the ruins a mile down the road. I wouldn't have noticed if Ann hadn't pointed it out. It was a clearing with a hole, a big rectangular one, with trees right in its middle. The hole was lined with stones.

"House foundation," said Ann. "The chimney is over there."

"Doesn't look like much," I said.

"But it does make you wonder about them, doesn't it?" she said. "Who they were. What they did . . . what happened to them."

"When you're dead, you're dead," said Uncle Dave.

32

9

"How much farther?" I asked.

"Maybe two miles."

We continued at a steady pace. Every now and again the army guns sounded in the distance like a reminder. I was edgy again. I felt that I was being watched. Uncle Dave, I noticed, kept stealing looks at me as if to catch me at something. I began wishing he hadn't come at all.

We went on. As we did, Uncle Dave's face became red, bright with sweat. "Didn't think it'd be so warm," he said, and took another rest.

That time we waited fifteen minutes before starting again.

Twice we passed foundations of old homes, the brown stone heavy and broken. In one of the places a tree had split a piece of stone, like a hand reaching out of time.

We plodded on.

Then Ann announced, "We're almost there."

Uncle Dave stopped, ran a handkerchief around

his face and neck, and looked at me as if asking for something. His face, which had been red, was now a chalky white.

"Water?" I offered.

"Take all you want," said Ann.

Uncle Dave took a swallow of water, coughed, then gave the canteen back.

Wanting to get there faster, I decided to take the lead. Ann, however, kept trying to slow me down— or so it seemed—by pointing out sights.

"Ruins of five houses in there. And see that?" she said. "It's an old turntable, where they turned the steam engines around. And right down there," she said, pointing, "is where we want to go."

"Where?"

"See the bridge? The Appalachian Trail passes next to it. We're only a quarter mile away from the cemetery."

"I'm sick," Uncle Dave announced.

10

He sat down on the ground by the roadside, breathing hard.

I stood there, not knowing what to do. Ann, however, immediately went to his side and knelt. "What is it?" she asked softly.

Uncle Dave shook his head. "I don't know," he said faintly. "Dizzy or something."

Ann offered the canteen. At first he shook his head, but when she persisted, he took a swallow. I stood there not sure what was going on, only that something was very wrong.

"Maybe we shouldn't have come," said Uncle Dave, watching down the road.

Ann glanced at me. "Take off your jacket," she said. "Roll it into a ball."

I did as she asked; then she took it, and with a gentle push against Uncle Dave's shoulder made him lie down, head resting on the improvised pillow.

His face was an awful white, as if his blood had gone bad. His eyes were closed.

Ann took off her jacket and put it over him. "Better to keep warm," she said.

Uncle Dave lay there perfectly still.

"Want some GORP?" Ann asked him.

He shook his head no.

"He going to be all right?" I asked. I was feeling guilty, remembering how I had wished him dead.

"I think so," she said, with a quick look at her watch. "Let's have lunch."

From her knapsack I pulled out the spread, a few sandwiches, fruit, some granola bars.

"Feel like eating?" she asked Uncle Dave. "It'll warm you up."

"Okay," he managed to say, but didn't move much.

I appealed to Ann with a look.

"He'll be okay," she said.

Reassured, I looked to see where we were. Down the road I could see the bridge. On either side the trees crowded in. There was hardly a sound. Yet at the same time it seemed as if I were hearing something, something like a hissing sound, something slipping through the trees. But nothing moved. There was no wind. Everything was still except for the guns thumping at a distance.

Uncle Dave sat up. Ann, giving support, knelt behind him. He sipped some more water.

When I turned around, he was watching me closely. But when our eyes met, he quickly turned away.

"Give him a sandwich," Ann urged.

I got one out. Uncle Dave took it, eating slowly. I gave another sandwich to Ann, took one for myself.

Then I just stood there, eating, my eyes searching the area.

There was another series of explosions from the military reservation.

"How far away are they?"

"Who's that?"

"Those army guys."

"Oh, maybe seven miles."

"They sound closer."

She shrugged.

We continued to eat in silence.

"I thought I'd be able to walk it," said Uncle Dave. His voice was firmer. "I suppose we'd better head back."

"What do you mean?" I asked. "Didn't you say it was only a little bit ahead?"

"Yes," said Ann.

"Then why can't we go?" I was angry.

"I'm too beat," said Uncle Dave with a shake of his head.

"I'm not." I turned away, frustrated.

Ann stood up. "You stay here," she said to me. "I'll get the van for him."

"Ann," I said, "I'm going to see it."

"You can't leave him alone."

"Did the two of you plan this?" I yelled.

"Plan what?"

"That we don't get there!"

"Are you kidding?"

"How long will it take me to get to the cemetery from here?"

"A few minutes."

"Then *you* wait. I'm going to see it."

"What about him?"

I gazed into the woods, down the road toward the bridge. I said, "He just doesn't want me to go!"

Her eyes widened.

Uncle Dave beckoned her over. When she reached him, he held up an arm. She grabbed his hand and helped him to his feet, then fetched his walking stick.

"I'm going on," I announced. I didn't care what happened to him.

Uncle Dave turned quickly. "Don't be a fool!" he said with strength.

"Isn't that why we came?" I shot back.

"Don't!" he said.

"Which way is it?" I asked Ann.

"John, we should get back . . ."

"Do what you want!" I turned and left them, heading for the bridge.

II

Made of stone, the bridge was an old one, though it looked as if it had recently been repaired. It crossed a deep ravine, at the bottom of which was a small, bright stream.

On the near side was a wooden sign with painted letters: APPALACHIAN TRAIL.

My eyes followed the direction of the pointed arrow. A path led into the woods. Nothing more. As I stood before it, Ann and Uncle Dave came up, Uncle Dave moving fast.

"Which way?" I wanted to know.

"There," said Ann, indicating the path. She was staring at me.

"You two coming or not?" I asked.

Ann looked to Uncle Dave. He was standing there, both hands folded over the top of his walking stick, watching me. "It's a mistake," he warned me.

"Your idea," I returned.

His face became sad, tired. "Sorry I ever told you," he said.

I ignored that. "You?" I asked Ann.

"I'll stay with him," she said.

"Suit yourself," I said, and started to walk along the trail without looking back. But I hadn't gone more than fifty feet before Uncle Dave called.

"John! Wait!" And he started to follow. Ann hesitated, trying to make up her mind what to do. In the end she came too.

Not caring if they caught up, I continued to move down the trail. After our walk on the wide railroad bed it seemed very dark. Crowded by laurel bushes, the trees provided a thick canopy of leaves. With all that shadow, it was like walking a tightrope into a dark, narrow room.

I came into a clearing. Here there was grass, like a lawn. But no cemetery stones. Just the deep-cut foundations of a number of old houses.

Uncle Dave and Ann came up.

"Where's the cemetery?" I asked.

"Down there," said Ann. "This is the old town of Rausch. If you look carefully, you can find the remains of six houses."

Not caring at all about the old town, I moved toward the cemetery, only to find the trail split into two paths. By that time I was almost crazy with frustration. "Where?" I demanded.

Ann pointed.

I began to jog in the direction she indicated, my heart beating wildly. By the time I hit the cemetery, I was running full tilt.

12

It was a small area, some sixty by fifty feet, all grass, with the look of having been tended only rarely. There were nine gravestones, two larger than the others.

They were scattered about in no particular pattern. The two larger stones were tilted, almost falling.

I looked at the nearest stone, one of the small ones.

ELIZABETH ROWAN
47 Days
God Held Her Too Dear To Give Her Up
January 1853

A child's grave.

My eyes were drawn to the largest of the stones.

I stood before it, then squatted so I could make out the letters, which were partly covered with green lichens.

JOHN PROUD
August 1854
R.I.P.

My heart turned over. My own grave. My name. Standing there I felt split in two.

But as I stared the feeling faded. In its place came disappointment. The stone itself was not in any way frightening, or even interesting.

I went down on my knees to take a better look, then put out a hand and touched the chiseled letters. They were rough. The canteen got in my way. I took it off and laid it to one side.

"Find it?"

I jumped. Uncle Dave and Ann had arrived.

I caught a questioning look from Uncle Dave, though exactly what he was asking I didn't know.

"What's the big deal?" I said, standing up.

Ann, arms folded across her chest as if to keep warm, gazed about. "I don't like it," she said.

My disappointment increased. "This *is* his grave, right?"

Uncle Dave nodded.

Puzzled, feeling flat, I walked about a bit, looking

42

at the other stones. They were severely weathered, almost impossible to read. One was for a married couple. They shared the same date of death.

I turned back to Ann and Uncle Dave. They were already waiting for me to leave.

"We can go," I said, feeling cheated.

Uncle Dave gave what sounded like a sigh of relief. "Suits me," he said, and started to move out along the trail.

Ann and I walked out side by side. "You people sure made a big thing out of nothing," I said.

Head slightly bowed in concentration, arms still folded, Ann didn't speak.

"I thought it would be spooky, or scary. Nothing. It's better at the movies."

Ann looked up then and gave me a smile, a warm one. I let go with a grin of my own, wondering why I had been so crazy before. I had looked at a grave belonging to someone who had died more than a hundred years ago. Big deal! John Proud was nothing to me.

We reached the point where the trail had split. Uncle Dave was sitting on the ground resting and waiting, looking much better than he had before. My bad feelings about him had vanished.

For a moment we stood there as if undecided what to do next.

"Got some water?" asked Uncle Dave.

I reached for the canteen, only to remember that I had taken it off and left it in the cemetery. "Left it!" I said. "Be back in a minute," I called as I started off.

"Don't!" I heard Uncle Dave cry. "Don't!"

It was too late. I was running down the pathway toward the cemetery, glad to be moving, to be free.

In seconds I burst breathlessly into the cemetery. The canteen was there by John Proud's grave. And sitting atop the stone was a boy, a teenager, fairly tall, somewhat on the thin side. He looked like anybody and nobody, a perfectly normal-looking kid. But he was oddly familiar, like someone I had met once, yet could not quite recall.

"Hello, John," said the person. "My name is John Proud. The *first* John Proud. Delighted to meet you."

With a shock I realized why he looked so familiar. I was staring at a mirror image.

He was me.

PART TWO

13

I stood there, trying to take hold of what I was seeing.

"Who are you?" I found voice to say.

"John Proud," he repeated, extending an arm and offering to shake hands.

I took his hand, except there was *nothing* but a touch as brief as the breath it might take to blow out a small candle. It was as if the only way he could demonstrate that he existed was to show me he did not.

"When we get to know one another better, I'll be more . . . there," he said, as if reading my mind.

I backed off a few steps.

"Please," he said, "don't leave. There is a great deal to say and not much time."

"Who are you?" I asked again.

He returned, echolike, "Who are you?"

"John Proud," I said.

There was an easy laugh from him, along with a casual hand gesture. "Same for me. Don't I look familiar?"

I said nothing.

"You'd be amazed," he said, "how difficult it is for people to recognize themselves. Well, you've made a good start. You've noticed. I must say, I appreciate your uncle going to all this trouble getting you here."

"Uncle Dave?"

"I admit it. I've used him, but it was you I needed." The smile was gone.

"Why?"

"To give me shape, voice, *being*."

Not understanding, I shook my head.

"Look here, John," he said, as if reasoning with a child, "I *am* John Proud." He patted the side of the gravestone on which he was still sitting. "The one who's buried here. Believe me, not much is left. I need you."

"I don't want anything to do with you," I got out.

"Oh, but you *do*," he said. "You wanted to know all about me. Your namesake. Your relative. Your blood. That cousin of yours, that Ann, I tried to use her once. But I only managed to scare her away.

"And I tried your Uncle Dave when he was here before. But look at him, getting sick, changing his mind. No, not strong enough." He paused. "Didn't he tell you he spoke to me?" There was a mocking look on his face.

I shook my head no.

"Well, why should he? All the same, it was through him that I gained a sense of you, and it was you I needed. I've waited a long time for you, John. But here you are."

"I won't give you anything," I said.

"Say what you will," he replied. "It probably makes you feel better. Only listen to me, John: I would not be here now unless you wanted me."

I had wanted to come. I knew that. But had I wanted to meet *him*?

I swung about and started to leave.

"Don't you want to know what will happen?" he cried out.

He had not touched me. I'm not sure if, then, he could have. Nor did he *do* anything, or say anything to make me stay. Yet, at his question, I paused and turned.

"See?" he said, his voice gentle. "There's lots to know, isn't there? Why is this happening to me?

47

you're asking yourself. Is it true what he's saying? Oh, you've a fine, fine inquisitive mind. Lots of questions."

I don't know if those things were in my head before he spoke. When he said them, however, they seemed to become so. I *did* want to know. I faced him.

"Good," he said. "Now then, I want nothing from you, John, *nothing other than what you want to give me.* I don't intend to haunt you. Nothing of the kind! *You* are in control. Never forget that. Not me. *You.* All that happens will be *your* doing. *Your* wanting. Don't ever forget that, ever!"

"What will you do?" I stammered out.

"That's all up to you. You didn't want Ann's father along on today's hike. Done! Any thought of what I should do next?"

"Go back to where you came from!" I cried.

"How can I, John, when it was you who called me up?"

Angrily, I shook my head.

"I know," he said. "You'd rather think otherwise. You're a nice fellow. Considerate. Polite. Straightforward. Above all, honest. Everyone thinks so. Your friends. Your family. Ann. But somewhere in you, John, is something very different, isn't there? And that shall be a secret between us. I won't tell a soul."

"That's not true," I insisted, "it's not!"

"Too late!" he warned. "I am your secret, John. I shall never be a stranger to you again."

"I'll get rid of you!" I cried, advancing on him, fists clenched.

"There is only one way to do that, John, and you don't have the courage to . . ." But suddenly he vanished, vanished completely, leaving not a trace.

"John?" I heard. "John? Are you all right?"

I wheeled about. At the edge of the cemetery was Ann.

14

It was as if I had been caught doing something wrong—discovered stealing or worse. I felt ashamed.

"Did you find it?" she asked.

"What?" I said, not sure how much she had seen or heard.

"The canteen."

I had completely forgotten.

"It's right there," she said, pointing.

"Right," I said, glad for the excuse to turn away. Moving quickly, I picked it up. "Sorry to keep you waiting."

"You didn't. I just wanted to tell you about Cousin Dave. He looks better but he needs to take it easy."

"Whatever you say," I told her, relieved. I was sure she hadn't seen or heard anything.

We walked away from the cemetery in silence. My head was spinning, trying to grasp what had happened, at least what I thought had happened. It was all a jumble. Then too, I began to worry about Uncle Dave. What did *he* know?

He was sitting on the ground as we emerged from the trail. When he saw me, he gave me a long look. I offered him the canteen.

"We need to get you back home," said Ann.

"I'm fine," insisted Uncle Dave.

"Tell you what," said Ann to me, ignoring him. "Take my pack. You two can sit, or walk, whatever, long as you go slow. I'll run back to the van, then drive back in."

"Run?"

"Jog. It's only four miles. It'll save a lot of time."

"I'm perfectly all right," said Uncle Dave as he

got to his feet. But Ann had given me her stuff and was already trotting off. For a moment Uncle Dave and I just stood there, watching her go.

"Might as well start," said Uncle Dave.

I should have made him sit down and wait, but I felt almost panicky at the thought of being alone with him. Walking side by side would make things easier for me. If we had to talk, I didn't want to face him.

We started off, moving at a slow pace. From time to time he would glance at me as if expecting me to speak first. "What happened?" he finally asked, breaking the silence.

"Nothing."

"You went back."

"To get the canteen."

He stopped short and faced me. He put a hand on my arm to pull me around, forcing me to look at him.

At his touch all my anger toward him returned. Sharply, I shoved his hand away. "What did he give you to get me there?" I asked.

Startled, he opened his mouth. He gulped and stepped back. As I stood there watching him, he seemed to crumple. It was as if he was shrinking, becoming older.

He started to say something, but stopped himself.

We continued to walk on. I walked faster, making him work that much harder to keep up. Only once did he speak.

"I made a mistake," he murmured, but it was as much to himself as to me.

Within forty-five minutes Ann came in with the van.

We quickly headed out, me in the front with Ann, Uncle Dave lounging exhausted in the back, quickly nodding himself into a doze. I kept my eyes on the road.

I had met someone, or *something*. This . . . thing . . . who looked, talked, and acted like me, who was me, and yet . . . I reminded myself, who was as completely different as anyone could be from me. I recognized myself in all ways but one, and that one was his mind. It was not mine.

"John?" It took me a second to recognize Ann's soft voice.

I shook my head clear. "Sorry. I was watching the road."

"What's going on?" she asked.

Keeping my eyes before me, I felt myself tense. We were heading down, the curves of the road an almost perfect spiral. "What do you mean?" I asked, though I knew perfectly well what she was talking about.

"You're acting like you're in shock."

"Just worried about Uncle Dave. Think he's all right?"

"Probably pushed himself too far. Too much excitement. Do you drive?" she asked.

"Nope."

Again, silence.

"It was you I was asking about," she said, her voice low. "You went back for that canteen. When I found you there . . . something—"

"I told you," I insisted quickly. "I'm just worried about Uncle Dave."

"Okay," she said. Then, after a few moments, she said, "I thought, you know, you might have seen something. You're acting funny . . ."

"Am I?"

She glanced at me. "Like you were frightened of something."

I wanted to tell her everything that had happened, but I also wanted to get away, to run home where everything would be safe again.

"I told you it was a strange place," she said.

I didn't know how to begin. I nodded yes to her words. "You told me," I said, but I couldn't say more.

15

When we got back to Lickdale, the other Fentons were still gone. But Uncle Dave, awake, seemed revived. I was anxious to go. Instead, we sat around the kitchen table while he had some coffee.

It was about two o'clock in the afternoon when he announced he was ready.

"You sure you're up to it?" Ann questioned.

"Fit as a fiddle," he insisted.

"You could wait for my folks."

"No point. Besides, I'd rather drive in daylight."

Silently, Ann appealed to me. I shrugged, then gathered up our few things and put them into our car.

"Why don't you go by the Little League field and say good-by to my mom," Ann suggested. "I'll show you the way. She'll feel badly about not seeing you off."

"Don't want to bother her," said Uncle Dave.

Wanting only to leave quickly, I made up an excuse. "He promised to get me home early," I said. Ann threw me a look.

Uncle Dave went out to the car. Ann held me back. "I don't think you should go," she said flat out. "I don't think he's that well."

"I can't make him stay."

"Yes you can," she said. "Tell him it's not safe."

I held out my hand. "Thanks for your help."

"Will you at least call and let me know you got home all right?" she asked. Quickly, she wrote out their number on a piece of paper and handed it to me. "I'm worried about him."

"You sound like my folks."

She put a hand to my arm. "John, please, I don't think you should go."

Her touch made me hesitate. There was a beep of the car horn.

"I'll call," I said.

"I intend to worry till you do," she said, giving in with a smile.

"I take it back. You're worse than my folks."

That time she laughed.

"Call," she repeated as I left.

The day was still bright, but Uncle Dave didn't drive as fast as when we had come. He was quiet. No wisecracks. No teasing. No philosophy. He did make one effort to get me to talk. "Was the trip worth it?" he asked.

"Suppose."

He gave me a timid glance. Then after a while he said, "I need some coffee. I'm going to pull off at the next town." His face was drawn, flushed, like it had been on the trail.

"You feeling okay?" I asked, alarmed.

"Tired."

"Pull off."

He took the next exit, which had a couple of gas stations and a diner right there. We pulled into the diner's parking lot.

We got a booth right away, and a waitress took our orders. I had pie à la mode and a soda. He ordered more coffee.

While I ate he sipped at his drink, his eyes staring off into some distant place. As we sat there, my concern grew for having pushed him so much.

"Maybe we should go back to Lickdale," I offered.

He shook his head, took a couple of gulps, wiped a tearing eye with his fingers. His hand trembled. "Look," he suddenly said, "I need to tell you something."

I braced myself, afraid of what he might say, not certain I wanted to hear. Instead of speaking, he placed an arm on the table, pushed the mug away, and cradled his head. The next moment he slipped out of the booth and fell to the floor, unconscious.

* * *

Fortunately, there was a guy behind the counter who knew what to do. Some sort of volunteer fireman. After checking to see that Uncle Dave wasn't choking, he covered him so he would stay warm. Someone else, meanwhile, called an ambulance.

I called home. No one was there. My folks had gone away for the weekend, and I couldn't remember who they were visiting. Next I called Lickdale, using the number Ann had given me. She answered.

"Ann?" I said.

"What happened?" I told her about Uncle Dave.

"I knew you shouldn't have gone," she said. "How bad is he?"

"Don't know. They've called an ambulance."

"You okay?"

"Yes," I said.

"When you find out which hospital they're taking him to, call back," she said. "I'll wait by the phone. Mom should be here soon. We can get to where you are pretty fast."

By the time I got back to Uncle Dave, the ambulance had arrived. So had a police car.

While the medics were tending to Uncle Dave, the cop, a state trooper, talked to me. I gave him as much information as I had, which wasn't much.

When they got Uncle Dave into the ambulance, the trooper took me to his car and we followed. They were taking the old guy to the nearest hospital emergency room, but even before we got there, a radio report came through from the ambulance. "Acute exhaustion," they said.

"That all?" I said to the trooper.

"That's all they're saying."

The trooper would have stayed at the hospital, but I said he didn't need to, telling him that relatives were on their way. All the same he gave me a number to call as well as his name, making me promise to let him know how things worked out.

Soon as he left I called Lickdale. I gave Ann a report, including where we were. As we were talking, Nora came back. I spoke to her. She was very upset.

"Hang on," she told me. "We'll be there soon as we can."

There was nothing to do then but wait in an empty room with Muzak and some six-month-old magazines for company. As I just sat there, an awful notion was growing in my head: Whatever had happened to Uncle Dave, it had been my doing. The more I thought about it, the more certain I was that it was my fault. Over and over again it came, "I did it, I did it." But a second voice kept insisting it was not me. If anyone had done anything, it was *him*, the other John Proud. Not me. *Not me.*

16

When Nora arrived she gave me a big, comforting hug, then went right off to find someone who could give her some answers. Martin read a magazine. I slumped back into my chair. Ann stood in front of me, hands in the high pockets of her jeans.

"What's going on?" she asked quietly.

I lay back in the big, soft chair, my eyes closed.

"John," she persisted, "what happened out there?"

"Where?" I said, pretending not to understand.

"The cemetery. Something happened. Did you tell him about it?"

"Who?" I said, feeling immediate alarm.

"Cousin Dave."

I shook my head.

"You going to tell me?"

I said nothing.

Nora came back. "Exhaustion," she announced. "Pure and fortunately simple."

I sat right up. "They sure?"

"Absolutely. He just shouldn't have made that hike. It's like someone pulled the plug on his energy. Just gone. They say he'll be all right, but with his age they want to keep him under observation for a couple of days. Just a precaution. He's sleeping now. Why don't you try your parents again?"

I did, but still got no answer. "They weren't expecting me to be home till late tonight," I explained. "They went to visit some friends. I don't know who."

"Well, he can't be moved," said Nora. "And we won't get another report till late tonight, or early morning. I want you to come back with us, John. I'm sure your parents would rather you were there than here. We'll figure out the details later."

"What about his car?"

"Where is it?"

"At the diner."

"Remember the name? I'll call them and work out something."

She did, too, so we didn't have to worry about that. Then we went out to the Fentons' van and, without much talk, drove off.

It wasn't long before we saw a long line of army trucks moving east on the highway. They were in a single line, maybe forty of them, moving slowly with their headlights on even though it was still daylight. It made me think of a funeral procession.

"Looks like a war," I said.

"Week's army camp is over," explained Ann. "Tomorrow a whole new load of reserves come in."

With no one talking much I found myself sleepy, my head nodding.

"Go lie in the back," suggested Nora. "You must be beat."

I didn't argue. There was a sleeping pad in the rear section. I lay down and closed my eyes. The next thing I knew we were in Lickdale.

I tried my folks again, but still didn't get an answer. Then it was time for dinner. Tom Fenton came back and learned what had happened. He shook his head. "One thing after another," he said. I looked up sharply. Ann was watching me.

When I finally reached my parents, it was late. Naturally, they were shook. But when Nora got on the line they sorted it out. We would all meet the next morning at the hospital.

I went to sit out on the front steps, trying once more to clear my head.

After a while Ann came out and sat down next to me, penny whistle in hand. At first she said nothing. Then, "That first time I went up there, I got frightened. It was like . . . well, once I went to Philadelphia with my mom. At one point we split up.

61

Then when it was time to meet, I couldn't find her. I thought everyone was a mugger, or out to get me. You know, *everyone*. It turned out that Mom was just waiting on the opposite corner. But I sort of freaked out. . . . And up there, at the cemetery, where there was no one, John, I had the same panicky feeling. Like someone was going to . . . I don't know. Attack me."

I kept silent, not sure how I could even begin to explain.

"Why won't you tell me?" she finally said.

"Nothing to tell."

She sat awhile longer, then lifted the whistle and began to play. No sooner had she begun, however, than she changed her mind, got up, and without another word went inside.

I stayed alone, feeling miserable, wishing I had the courage to speak to her, to tell her what had happened. I really needed some answers.

That made me think about Uncle Dave. He had been about to say something before he collapsed. I wished I could find out what that was without having to see him. He made me too uncomfortable. Then I began to wonder if he would talk to anyone else about me, about John Proud. Would they believe him? Maybe they would think he was just crazy. I found myself wishing that he would just . . . disappear, be gone.

My thoughts were interrupted by the sound of booming over the military range. It made me ask myself how anyone could live with that racket so near, so constant.

Then I remembered: There wasn't supposed to be anything that night. Hadn't they told me the army people had gone home? I must have misunderstood. At the thought, the gun firing faded away.

I made up my mind that I would face up to Uncle Dave, ask him what he knew, then make him promise not to tell anyone.

I tried to figure out exactly what Uncle Dave knew about me that I didn't. All that talk about *evil* . . . his hints. The thought of his teasing brought my anger back. Hadn't John Proud pretty much said he had made a deal of some kind with Uncle Dave to get me to the cemetery? Talk about *evil* . . .

And what had I done? Pushed him so hard he collapsed.

So it went, back and forth, rage one moment, guilt the next. Finally I went to bed. Even then I spent a lot of time staring up into the darkness. My last thought of the day: I wished Uncle Dave would just . . . go away.

Early the next morning we drove back to the hospital.

As we pulled into the parking lot, the first thing I saw was my folks' car. Right away my heart sank, wondering if they had gotten to Uncle Dave, and if he had told them what had happened, really happened.

But at the door when I saw their faces, I knew instantly something else had happened. Sure enough, they told us: During the night Uncle Dave had died.

17

It was as if my *thinking* had made it happen. Hadn't I wanted him out of the way? Hadn't I wished him to disappear? And to tell the truth, I felt a ghastly relief on hearing the news. I shoved that relief away, fast and deep, deep as I could, telling myself I hadn't meant it, not really.

In the sudden confusion my eyes searched out Ann. Her eyes were right on me. Across that hall we tried to read each other's thoughts. She was no longer asking me *if* anything had happened at the cemetery. She wanted to know *what*. I turned away quickly. The whole thing was over and done with. All I needed to do now was keep my mouth shut for John Proud to go away.

"Should I call you, or will you call me?" she said before we left.

"I'll call," I said.

"Promise?"

"Yes," I said, but I knew I never would.

Before we left I talked to the doctor who had tended Uncle Dave. "Sir," I said, "I was the one with my uncle when he got sick."

He turned to look me over. That examining glance brought new fears. Maybe people could look at me—the way Uncle Dave had done—and see something wrong. I had a flash of memory about that history teacher saying that people could *see* that something was wrong. What did they see?

All the doctor said was "Sorry about all this. It must have been very hard for you."

I got up my courage. "Was it just exhaustion?"

"Old age mostly. Something just went out of him."

"Like what?"

"Just an expression," he said, looking at me. "Did you have something in mind?"

65

"I don't know," I said, "maybe . . . something . . . I did."

"You?" He put a hand to my shoulder. "There was nothing you could have done. Nothing. It was his idea to go on that hike, wasn't it? People do what they want and take the consequences."

There was that word again—want. What did *I* want? I wondered.

18

The funeral was held three days later. People, mostly family, kept coming up to me, consoling me. I was afraid to look anyone in the face. Maybe they would guess the truth. Just as they were lowering the coffin, I once more felt that strong sense of relief. I heard myself think, "I'm glad. It's done with. It's over."

Those thoughts shook me with shame. Tears gathering, I hung my head. My father, thinking I was showing grief for Uncle Dave, put a comforting arm around me. That made it even worse.

Over the next two weeks I kept more and more to myself. I didn't feel comfortable with people, especially my friends. My excuse was that I had to study, that I needed to get good grades. The end of the term was fast approaching. I was left alone.

Not that staying home was easy. Restless, I started to take long walks, meandering through streets, malls, shopping centers, just looking at things. Half the time I didn't know what I was doing.

Often my thoughts were of Ann. I missed her, but thinking of her made me think of the whole John Proud business, and I was trying to forget that. So I tried not to think of her either. Still, in my walks I would think of things to get her, like a special running outfit, or a recording of some music that reminded me of her penny whistle. Not that I bought anything.

Once, when I was looking at a fancy compass that I thought would be good for hiking, I felt a sudden urge to steal the thing. I was so startled by the thought that I all but dropped the compass and fled from the store.

The truth was that I did spend a lot of my time going over what had happened at the cemetery in St. Anthony's Wilderness. How many times I visited the place in my head I don't know. Over and over again. There were times I felt I was actually there.

Perhaps I was.

19

One Saturday morning after about two weeks, I got a call.

"Hi. It's Ann."

"Oh, hi," I said, my heart doing a flip.

"I was hoping you'd call," she said in her best direct way. "You okay?"

"Sure," I replied.

"What's that supposed to mean?"

"Means I'm all right."

"Things settle down?"

"I guess."

"You don't seem very certain."

"Sorry I didn't call," I said.

"That's okay. But why didn't you stop by when you were around last weekend?"

"What?"

"You were in town last weekend. You might have stopped by to say hello. Mom was upset. So was I. She thinks your parents blame her for what happened to Cousin Dave. Is that why you didn't come by?"

I shook my head clear. "What makes you think I was there?"

"Martin saw you at the gas station. He even said hello. You talked to him."

"I wasn't there," I said.

"What do you mean?"

"I've been here, home, all the time."

"John, Martin spoke to you. You spoke to him. Not very nicely, he said, but it was you. And you said you were going up to the cemetery."

"Ann," I said after a moment, "I'm telling the truth. I wasn't there."

She said nothing.

"Did Martin see who I was with?" I asked.

"Well, no, I guess not. No one else."

"Alone?"

"Well, he saw you get into a car and go off alone."

"Ann, I don't drive. I don't have a license."

There was a long silence. "I guess he made a mistake," she said. "Didn't mean to be so sore. But you did say you'd call, and I guess I was upset when I thought you didn't want to see me. *Is* everything all right?"

"I think so," I answered carefully. My mind was racing. "How are things there?" I asked automatically.

"School's out," she said. "Only a lot of funny

69

things have been happening around here. Stuff being ripped off. The sheriff's office is calling it a crime wave. That's one theory. The other is that it's just one thief. Not that anyone has ever seen the person. There's talk about a teenage curfew."

"Too bad," I mumbled, feeling a renewed sense of panic as I remembered my wanderings through malls, shopping centers, my urge to steal the compass. All I could think of was John Proud.

"You're not going to tell me what happened, are you?" she said.

"What do you mean?"

"You know."

I took a breath, wanting so much to talk to her, to tell it all, to say that it was probably John Proud who had talked to Martin, that he was the "crime wave." But I was the one who had brought him back, wasn't I? So it was my fault. How could I tell her that?

"Are you going to talk to me?" I heard her say.

"I can't now," I said. "My dad is standing right here. But I promise . . . I'll call."

"When?"

"Soon."

"Really?"

"Really."

I hung up, knowing I had no intention of calling

at all, ever. I wanted to get away from the whole thing, all of it. As far away as possible. And that included Ann.

I lay down on my bed and listened to the empty house. Then I buried my face in my pillow, just holding on. I had one thought: If only I had some money, real money, I would go someplace where no one could find me. No one.

20

The last week of school I tried to keep my mind on what I had to do, on taking final exams. It wasn't easy. Once, in fact, I had a real scare.

I was walking down the street near where I lived, not thinking about anything in particular. All of a sudden I looked up and saw this person walking right toward me. I kept walking. The person kept walking. Increasingly, he seemed familiar, as though I knew him, knew him well. But I couldn't place him. Then, with a shock, I realized it was someone who looked exactly like me. Stopping short, I felt my heart leap. Was it *him*? The next second I realized that it was only a mirror, a mirror that someone had left outside, leaning against a box.

I stood there on the sidewalk and for the first time—then and there—I tried to truly confront the facts.

I had come face to face with a spirit, a demon, *something* that wasn't of the world. That something had taken my shape, borrowed it so to speak. It had begun to act on me in ways I didn't fully understand. Worse, it had entered my thoughts, making me think horrible things, and then it acted them out, made them happen as if they were *my* doing. But they weren't.

The night before my last exam, I was trying hard to study when the phone rang. My mother called that it was for me. I went to the phone.

"John?"

"Yes."

"Ann."

"Oh, hi. How are you?"

"How you been?" she asked. I caught the tension in her voice. Something was very wrong.

"I'm fine," I said. "My last exam is tomorrow. Spanish. What's up?"

She paused for just a moment as if getting the strength to leap to something. Sure enough, it came

72

out in a burst. "Have you been around here lately?"

"Me?"

"Just tell me honestly," she said. "It's important. I have to know."

"No. Of course not. I've been in school. Here. Why should I be out there? I would have told you."

"Remember when I said Martin met you?"

"I wasn't there either."

"That's what you said."

"I wasn't, Ann!"

"John," she said, "remember I told you there had been a whole series of things . . . you know, things being stolen . . . all that?"

"Yeah."

"The other day, right here in town, someone tried to break into the Agway store. Where I work. He broke in at night. Only the manager came back for something, so he almost caught the guy. He was trying to steal money from the vault."

The moment she said that, I remembered my thoughts about wishing I had money. "Did they . . . catch him?"

"No. But he got a good look at him. And he described him to the police. I was working there when the police interviewed him. Well, the description . . ." She didn't finish.

73

I spoke what was in my head. "The description fit me."

"How did you know?"

"I guessed," I said, quickly sorry I had said anything.

"John, it . . . wasn't you . . . was it?"

"No." My heart was really racing.

"John, who is it? What's happening? You must tell me."

I took a breath. "Why?"

"Because I care about you!" she burst out. "Something has happened to you and I want to help. John, you're in trouble. You came here to see us and we talked, talked a lot. It made me feel good. We seemed . . . close. I care about you a lot. Let me help."

I closed my eyes and let her words sweep over me. I needed help. And she was offering. "John Proud," I said.

"I don't understand. That's you."

"No, Ann. The first one. The dead one."

Silence.

"I don't know what you're talking about . . ."

"I mean it."

"That's . . . crazy."

"I saw him, Ann. Spoke to him."

Silence.

"That time at the cemetery. *That's* what happened. That's what I didn't know how to tell you."
Then, "Ann, you still there?"

"I heard you." Her voice sounded hard.

"I'm sure it was him who got to Uncle Dave. He made Uncle Dave bring me to the cemetery."

"Why?"

"I'm not altogether sure," I said, my courage faltering. "But . . . he killed Uncle Dave."

"And you're serious?" There was something of awe in her voice.

"Yes."

For a moment I felt a flush of pride in the thought that I was in the middle of the whole affair, the center.

"That's terrible," she said. "What are you going to do about it?"

My moment of pride collapsed. In panic, I said, "I don't know," and hung up the phone.

I waited there, wanting her to call back. I wanted her to. She didn't, and I didn't have the nerve to pick up the phone myself. She had said I had to do something and she was right. It wasn't enough to just face the fact that John Proud was not going to let me go. I had to do something, quickly, before it got worse.

21

People act all kinds of ways when they are frightened. My way was to hide it.

With school out, the easiest thing for me to do was keep to myself. At first I got calls, friends trying to get together, asking where I was, what I was doing. I found excuses. Three mornings a week I went to a hardware store—the woman who ran it was a friend of my mother's. I did odd jobs, sweeping, inventory. It put some money in my pocket.

Besides that I watched TV a lot, read, stayed in my room, and slept. I felt tired all the time. After a while my friends didn't bother to call.

I kept wishing that Ann would call.

Another two weeks went by. It was July and hot with a humidity that had most people gasping, sticking close to their air conditioners.

I was home that Saturday night alone. My folks had gone out. There was no one I wanted to see. No one had called me for a couple of weeks.

Bored with TV, I went out to sit on our front steps

76

and watched the play of heat lightning up in the sky. It made me remember sitting with Ann in front of her house in Lickdale, feeling good about myself, about her. I knew I wanted to be with her, talk to her, be close. I really missed her.

Next morning she called.

"John?"

"How you doing?" I said. My voice shook.

"Not so good."

"What's the matter?"

Instead of an answer there was a long pause. For a moment I thought she'd hung up.

"What is it?" I asked.

"I'm upset," she said. I could sense then how shaken *she* was, almost as if she had been crying.

"Why?"

"You have to come here. You have to."

"What happened?"

"All this stuff . . ." She had been crying. And she was on the edge of it again.

"Please tell me what happened."

"I told you before, or wanted to . . . only you hung up on me."

"I'm sorry. I was upset."

"I'm trying to help you!" she cried out.

"Just tell me what it is."

"Remember," she said, "how there were all these

things happening, and how someone . . . someone saw a person who looked like you breaking into the Agway store . . ."

"It wasn't me, Ann . . ."

"And I believed you," she said. "But last night, late, I was coming home from a party. Driving. Alone. It wasn't *that* late. Anyway, I saw someone on the road, hitchhiking. Just standing on the road, you know, thumbs up, under a road lamp. I wasn't going to pick him up. I wouldn't. I kept going. But as I passed him, I looked. You know the way you do? Only it was you, John. It was. *I saw him.*"

Right away I remembered my thoughts of her the night before, how I wanted to be with her. "What did you do?" I asked.

"I wasn't going to do anything, right? But when I saw that it was . . . you . . . I had this automatic reaction. I put on my brakes. I mean, if you had seen me on the road in the middle of the night, wouldn't you have stopped?"

"Yes."

"Well, I did. And I turned to look around at him. I had gone past him a ways. You know the way hitchhikers run up to the car that's stopped. Well, I watched him come. He didn't run. He just walked, easy, as if he had all the time in the world, as if what he wanted most was for me to just see him.

78

But when I did—my parking lights are red—he came into view with this . . . this red cast about him, looking like a . . . devil. I knew it was only my car lights . . . but all the same . . . Anyway, it was you. *Exactly* like you. No way anyone else. He kept walking toward me, smiling, that same kind of nice, easy smile you have . . .

"I was thinking, what's John doing out here like this? But you know, I was really glad, excited it was you. I leaned over my seat to throw the door open when I suddenly realized what I was doing, and who you might be.

"I got going fast. Very fast. He just stood there looking after me.

"When I got home, I thought I should tell someone, but . . . I couldn't. So I went to bed and just lay there thinking and thinking and thinking until I decided I'd call.

"John," she said, taking a big breath. "What's happening?"

"I don't know," I said.

"So many things . . . I know what you told me. I believe it. Except I don't understand." She was crying. I didn't know what to say.

"John," she said, "you have to come here."

"Why?" I said.

"Because this is about you. It has to be you

79

who does something. Will you come?"

"I'll try," I said, not sure whether I meant it or not.

"John," she said after a moment.

"What?"

"We like each other, don't we?"

"Yes."

"Why won't you talk straight to me?"

"I'm having enough trouble talking straight to myself," I said evasively.

"I'm going to trust you," she said.

"Thank you," I managed. But in my head I knew I wasn't trusting *her* enough. "I hope you can," I said.

"Why do you say that?"

"Ann," I cried in exasperation, "when I spoke to John Proud, he said *I* got him to come back. That he was me!"

"Do you believe that?"

"Ann, I don't know."

For a moment she said nothing. "I don't," she said. "But I still think it's you who has to do something."

I knew more than ever that what she had said was right. I had to get out there and face John Proud.

I had to know who was doing all these things. Was it him . . . or me?

PART THREE

22

It was about six o'clock on a Thursday evening when I got to Lebanon. I was tired, feeling dirty and hungry. When I stepped from the bus there was Ann, waiting. She had dressed up a bit, slacks and all, though she was wearing her running shoes. She looked good.

I was so glad to see her, I just dropped my bag and we hugged each other hard. I was with the one person who knew some of what was locked up in my head. Secrets, I had learned, have weight.

"Want to stop for some coffee or something before we go back?" she asked. "Mom said she'd have dinner waiting."

"I'd like to talk."

"There's a McDonald's on the way."

"Fine."

When we got there, we ordered a couple of shakes, then slipped into one of those back booths with the hard, orange seats.

We looked at each other. "I was worried you might not come," she said.

I took a deep breath. "So was I. I'm glad to see you," I said. She smiled. "How much do your parents know?" I asked.

"Nothing, really."

I felt a trickle of worry. "Martin have any idea?"

"I doubt it. Anyway, he's going to Scout camp tomorrow."

"Can you get your parents to go too?"

She grinned, shook her head.

"Why do they think I've come?"

"Hot-and-heavy romance."

"My folks too. Fact they think all the stuff I've been doing—sticking around home, not seeing people, stuff like that—is because of you."

Then we just sat back and looked at each other, feeling good, a deep and easing warmth. Across the table we held hands.

"Have you got any answers yet?" she asked.

I shook my head. "Just questions."

"Like what?"

I hesitated.

"You going to trust me or not?" she asked, giving my hand a squeeze.

"I'm trying. . . ."

"Tell me. . . ."

I looked right at her. Her trust seemed to clear my mind, make it easier to speak. I took another deep breath. "I think . . . John Proud . . . is somehow . . . getting to be part of me. Not really me," I hastened to say. "But all the same, something *in* me."

Ann was watching me closely.

"It's like . . . he is me, but all the same, he's not. Doesn't make much sense, does it? It's as if he does things, things I might only think of doing. But I don't know if I'm the one who *is* thinking them."

"Who else?"

"Him. Putting thoughts into my head."

"Breaking things? Stealing?"

I nodded, adding, "Killing Uncle Dave."

She grimaced, gripping my hand harder.

"A lot of the things that you said were happening around here—well, I thought of them, *first*. They were in my head, Ann, they were."

"That's *not* you," she said almost angrily.

"I don't know anymore. I'm all confused about it."

She took her hand from mine.

"Tell me," she again urged. "I'm not going to think badly of you. I won't. I promise."

"I wanted Uncle Dave to disappear, Ann. I did. Maybe worse. I thought about stealing things. Thought about getting a lot of money. Or, that night you saw *him*, I wanted to see you a lot. More than usual, though I tried not thinking about you."

"Why?"

"I don't know," I admitted. "You're a part of this whole thing. The point is, I don't always know which are my thoughts, and which are his.

"Maybe he comes to exist through me, you know, a thought of mine . . . then he takes over. I don't *do* anything. I think things. He does them. Or maybe it's more: Maybe *he* puts those thoughts into my head, then does them to make me believe I'm the one to blame when it's really him all along.

"I don't know anymore. I used to know myself. Or I thought I did. Not anymore. I've never been this way before."

"What do you think you'll do about him?" she said.

"I'm not sure there either. All I can think of is

that I have to catch him. Get rid of him. I don't know how. But there has to be a way. He hinted there was a way."

"Do you want to kill him?"

I nodded. "Except he's already dead, isn't he?" She wrinkled her nose, and in spite of myself I started to laugh. "It's so crazy," I said, shaking my head.

"Maybe we're the crazy ones," she said. That wasn't funny either, but it set us off again.

"Can you imagine," she said, giggling, "telling my girl friend that I like this guy but there are two of them and I can't tell which one is which sometimes?"

I sobered up. "But there is something else," I said.

"What?"

"Look, Ann, if he's my opposite, and if I'm trying to get rid of him . . . well, see, this is one of the big questions: Doesn't it figure he's trying to do the same thing to me, you know, get rid of me?"

Her eyes grew wide with alarm. "What do you mean?"

"Ann," I said, and by that time we were holding each other's hands tightly, as if afraid to let go, "he wanted me to come here. Right? He got Uncle Dave to bring me. Okay, he's been doing all these things, this vandalism, thefts, you know . . . showing himself so that people will think it's me. And then, see, finally, he shows himself to you. That worked. He got me to come, right? Through you."

She had a look of horror on her face.

"If you look at it that way," I said, "so far he's winning. And if he's winning, then I'm losing, Ann. Losing fast."

23
_____

We drove in silence toward her house.

"Do you want to tell my parents?" she asked.

"No," I said softly.

"Why?"

"They won't believe it."

"John, they like you. And since what you're saying is true, they'll believe you."

"What if they don't?"

"They will."

"Maybe they would tell me to get out, tell you not to have anything to do with me. Even, you know, turn me in."

"What are you talking about?"

"Did you forget? The police must be looking for me. That place where you work, you said your boss or somebody discovered John Proud at his safe, right? And he gave a description of him to the police. You said you were there. Who fits that description?"

"But it wasn't you. . . ."

"And it wasn't me looking for a ride at night, either, was it?"

She shook her head.

I didn't say anything else, just looked out the window. We were passing through a succession of small towns surrounded by ripe farmland. It was all soft, easy, peaceful and safe-looking. But up ahead I could see the range of mountains that contained John Proud's grave. The mountains were dark and heavy, and it was there—I just had this feeling— that I'd meet him again. As we drove, those mountains loomed larger, and darker, all the time.

"I still think we should tell my parents," said Ann. "But if—" She stopped in mid sentence and sat up a little straighter in her seat. I pulled myself up to look down the road. Ahead was a bunch of red lights. Police cars were off to one side of the road and state troopers were getting cars to stop. A roadblock. I swore. Ann gave me a worried look.

"See what I mean?" I said.

There were about six cars in front of us. A state

trooper was working his way down the line. I tried to decide if I should make a run for it. I swore again. "There I am, telling you how tricky this was going to be, and we drive right into a trap."

"He's talking to the drivers," she whispered. "When he comes here, look out the other way."

It took about fifteen minutes for the trooper to reach us. We could see drivers passing out their papers. Ann told me to get out her insurance card from the glove compartment while she got her own stuff ready. "It'll make things go faster," she said.

The cop was crisp, polite, and hard. Not a wrinkle on his steel-gray uniform, and it was July, and though late in the day, still hot.

As he approached, I kept my face averted.

"Sorry to trouble you, miss. We're doing a check. May I have your license, registration, and insurance card please."

Ann handed them over. "What's the matter?" she asked.

The trooper didn't say. He took the papers, then walked slowly to the back of the car, matching the license plate with the registration card. Then we heard him use his hand radio to call in the information. He kept the box to his ear while they gave him a report.

Ann sat perfectly still, hands clasped in her lap.

I kept my eyes everywhere but where the trooper was.

Finally the trooper walked back to her side of the car, bent down, and handed back her stuff.

"These are fine," he said. Then, answering her question from before, he said, "We're looking for someone. Had a report he was in the area. Nothing for you to worry about. It's perfectly safe. Just don't pick up any hitchhikers." He tapped the window frame. "Everything's fine."

Perhaps it was his reassuring voice. Because despite my intentions, I turned around to look at him. I recognized him right away—the same trooper who had helped when Uncle Dave collapsed.

"Hi!" he said to me. "You're the one with the sick uncle. How're you doing?"

"Fine, sir."

"You promised to call me and tell me what happened."

"I forgot."

"I got word he died."

"Yes, sir."

"Sorry to hear that." He was staring at me, looking at my face with interest.

"Yeah," I said softly.

"Can we go?" asked Ann.

The trooper hesitated.

"You from around here?" he asked me.

"Philadelphia."

"Visiting?"

"Yes, sir."

"With you?" he said to Ann.

"We're relatives," she said.

"Right." He seemed unable to make up his mind. "Okay. Take it easy now. Drive carefully. Sorry to hold you up." He backed away from the car.

Ann started the motor and edged the car forward. Afraid to turn about, I looked at the rearview mirror. The trooper was standing behind us, not going on to the next car, but just watching after us. As we picked up speed, I kept my eyes on him. He had turned on his hand radio and was using it.

We passed three police cars. A few of the troopers were standing around talking to one another.

Ann accelerated as much as she dared.

At first we didn't say anything. My heart was pounding.

"What is it?" Ann said to me.

"He was onto me. I'm sure he was!"

"It was only about Uncle Dave. . . ."

"Maybe. But that's not what I'm worried about."

"Then what?"

"Look, I'm sure John Proud wants me up in those

mountains. He wants me. Do you think he'll let anything, or anyone, stop me from getting there?"

She looked at me sharply.

"It's not me I'm worried about," I said. "I'm safe. So far. It's that cop, or anyone, who tries to stop me. What's going to happen to them?"

Even as I said that, we heard the faint wail of a police siren.

24

I twisted around to look out the back window, but though the wail was growing louder, I couldn't see anything. Down the road, in front of us, was a cross-roads.

"Make a left!" I suddenly cried to Ann.

She applied the brakes, spun the wheel, and made a sharp turn.

"Pull over there!" I said, pointing straight ahead where there appeared to be a dip in the road and tall bushes right by the roadside.

She did what I said.

"Now, just sit."

She turned the key. The motor died. Then she leaned back in the seat, her head tilted against the headrest, her eyes closed.

Behind us we could hear the siren rising. I clasped my hands, pressing my palms hard together. I bit my lip. The siren's shriek reached a peak, then began to fade. It was soon gone.

Ann leaned forward and rested her forehead against the steering wheel. She shook her head.

"This is insane," she whispered.

I said nothing.

"How'd you know this was a good place to hide?"

"I don't know," I admitted, suddenly realizing what I had done. "I just knew it."

"The way you knew he was after you?" she said.

"He was."

"*How* did you know?"

I shook my head. "I just did."

She watched me intently. "What would have happened if he'd caught you?"

"I told you. He wouldn't. Something would have happened to him, something to keep him from reaching me."

"You're very sure, aren't you?"

I nodded.

"Can we go home now?"

"I don't know. I bet that's where he's going. If he

is, he'll be waiting for us. And he'll be talking to your folks too." I shook my head. "I don't want that."

She sat up and looked at me. "John, I'm not doubting you . . . but . . . we can't go along with just the way you *feel*. . . . Things are real, or they aren't. When we get to the house . . . I want you to promise me we'll talk to my parents. Please. Tell them what's happened, what you think. Trust them."

"Why?"

"Because they can help."

"If they're there," I said, at the same time hoping they wouldn't be.

"Where else would they be?" she said, and with a weary gesture she started up the car.

We went back to the crossroads, made a left, and headed for her home. "I won't go the way I normally do," she announced. "We'll take some back roads."

"I thought you didn't believe me."

"I don't know what to think anymore." Settling back into her seat, she stepped up our speed. Putting out a hand to one side, she touched me. "It's just so hard to think about all this."

"I know."

We drove in silence. There were very few cars on the road. The time of day, just before dusk, seemed to give a soft tone to everything. We seemed to be floating between two worlds. Up ahead the road, still radiating the hot day's sun, made the air tremble.

As we moved along, I began to think more and more about her parents. How would they react when I told them? I didn't want to. If only, I began to think . . . I froze, panic rising. I tried to concentrate on the road, on the car, on anything. But the thought came anyway. I didn't want to see her parents, I didn't want them to be there, only Ann and me there, just Ann and me. . . . I was bathed in sweat. I stole a glance at Ann. She smiled. I reached out and took her hand.

"How much farther?" I asked after a while.

"Twenty minutes."

Five minutes later we heard another siren. Ann slowed down, trying to decide from which direction the sound was coming.

In moments we rounded a bend in the road. A white-and-gold ambulance rushed into view, its red top light flashing.

Quickly, Ann moved over to one side to give the ambulance room. As it flashed by, we saw that it was being closely followed by a state trooper's car. We looked at each other.

I felt sick.

25

We drove into Lickdale at low speed. Ann pulled into the driveway. It was empty. No van.

"I thought my folks would be home," she said.

She parked. I reached for my suitcase and we got out. She opened the house door. It hadn't been locked. A hall light was on. We stood there, Ann listening intently.

"Anyone home?" she called.

No answer.

"Mom!" she cried. "Dad! Martin!" Her voice rose with increasing urgency.

"I'm here" came a soft voice. Martin came into the hall from the darkened living room, glassy-eyed from watching TV.

"Hi," he said. He looked puzzled to see us.

"Where is everyone?" Ann asked him.

"I'm here."

"Mom? Dad?"

"They went to get John."

"What do you mean?"

"He called and said you weren't there. Could they come and pick him up."

"When was that?"

" 'Bout half an hour ago."

"But he's here with me," said Ann. "I did pick him up."

Martin shrugged.

The phone rang, startling us.

"I'll get it," said Martin, and made a move toward the kitchen.

"Don't!" cried Ann.

Martin spun about.

"It'll be for me," she said, trying to recover. Her face ashen, she hurried to the kitchen. I followed closely.

Martin, sensing that something bad was happening, came too.

The phone kept ringing.

Ann reached for it, hesitated for a moment, then put the receiver to her ear, listening. Her eyes closed. "This is Ann Fenton," she said. "Their daughter."

I turned away. I didn't want to hear.

"Yes," said Ann softly. "I understand. Yes, I do. I can drive. No, that's all right. I understand. I will. Right here. Thank you." She put the phone on the hook.

"Who was that?" asked Martin, his voice small.

"The police," said Ann. "There's been an accident. Mom and Dad. They've been hurt."

26

The details didn't seem to matter. What it came
down to was that Nora and Tom had gone off the
road, their van landing in a ditch. Both of them
were shook up—Nora with a gash on her forehead,
Tom knocked out, a busted arm. It could have been
a lot worse. If anything, it was the van that had
suffered the most.

How had it happened? They had gotten the call,
presumably from me. They set out right away, worried too about Ann's whereabouts. They were speed-
ing. Suddenly Tom had to swerve to avoid someone
who had darted out onto the road. Nora claimed
she never did see anyone. Whoever the person was,
it wasn't he who reported the accident. It was the
state trooper who found them.

Ann wanted to get into the car fast and get down
to the hospital, but she called first. To her great
relief she was able to speak to her folks. Her parents
decided that the most helpful thing would be for

everyone to stay put. Martin, reassured by talking to his parents, agreed to go off to Scout camp the next morning as planned. Ann would drive him to the hospital to say good-by. Then she would take him to the Scoutmaster's house. Nora and Tom needed to stay in the hospital for at least two days.

By eleven-thirty that night Martin was fast asleep, and Ann and I were sitting in the kitchen feeling exhausted.

"Now what?" she said.

"You know who it was who called them, and who it was who jumped out in front of the van, don't you?" I said.

"Him," she said after a moment.

"I'll bet you anything that that trooper who found them was coming after me."

"John, did *you* think it? Did *you* want something to happen to them? I have to know."

"No. Not that way. I mean, I didn't want to talk to them or have them here. But not like *that*!"

"Did he make you have those thoughts, or was it you?"

"I didn't want them to get hurt, Ann, I didn't."

Her eyes filled with tears. Then she laid her head down on her arms.

"Would you rather I left?" I asked.

"No."

"It could get worse."

"How?"

"I don't know. I don't know what I think anymore."

She stared at me. "What does he want?"

"Me."

"What do you want?"

"To get away from him."

"He doesn't care what he does to people, does he?"

I shook my head.

"What do you think will happen when you do find him?"

"I don't know that either."

She got up out of her chair and leaned over the sink to look out the window into the dark night. "Sometimes," she said, "I have crazy thoughts. Weird ones. Mean ones. Small and stupid. Things that surprise and embarrass me. Things I would die rather than have people know were in my head. It's uncomfortable—worse—having them."

I felt my tension rising.

She wrapped her arms around herself. "Maybe people *should* have those kinds of crazy thoughts. It's not that you have to *do* them. Maybe if you deny them, don't allow them into your head, then they actually happen, happen in the worst way." For a moment she paused.

"Ann . . ." I felt suffocated.

"You didn't want my parents around."

I bowed my head. "It's him . . ." I insisted.

She said nothing at first. Then, "Do you know how you're going to find him?"

"I'll go back up to the cemetery. It seems the logical place to start, anyway."

"Just go?"

I nodded yes. "You can drop me off at the start of the trail. I can find it myself."

"You can't do that."

"Why?"

"You don't know how long you'll be there."

"Doesn't matter."

"It does. You said yourself you don't know what's going to happen. It might even take a few days."

"What else am I supposed to do?" I felt near to tears. "I have to go. Do you want him here?"

She thought for a while. "I'll go with you. I've got all the camping gear we need. John, I've been out there for as long as a week. I know what to do. I'll be able to help."

"No," I said. "I don't think you should."

"Why?"

"Look what he's done already!"

"No," she said, coming to a decision. "I'm not going to let you go alone."

"No telling what might happen."

"I know."

The house was very still.

She looked at the clock. "I have to get up early. They'll let us into the hospital at eight. Martin has to be at his Scoutmaster's at nine-thirty, latest."

She showed me to the guest room, where I had been the last time I was there. She looked around. "You should have everything you need." She started to go.

"Ann . . ." I said.

"What?"

"I'm sorry . . . about all this."

"So am I."

Then we just reached out and hugged each other. We stayed that way, maybe for a full minute. "Thank you," I said. She turned her face slightly, gave me a kiss by my ear.

"Get some sleep," she said, and quickly left.

27

I got undressed slowly, climbed into bed, and turned out the light. But I couldn't sleep. Once I heard the cannons, a short series, like exclamation points in the dark. I kept tossing, trying to find a comfortable place.

There was a slight tapping on the door.

"Yes?"

The door opened. It was Ann. She had her white bathrobe around her.

"I can't sleep," she said, leaning against the doorframe.

"Neither can I."

She made her way to the bed and sat down. After a moment I reached out and took her hand. We stayed that way—not speaking—for what seemed a long time.

"You want me to stay, don't you?" she said.

"Yes."

"I keep thinking about what you've been saying. Your thoughts. His thoughts. You don't really know which is which, do you?"

We remained motionless, though in my head I kept wanting her to stay, wanting her.

She gave my hand a squeeze. "I've thought about it too," she said. "It's what I'd like. But you don't know for sure whose thought you have, his or your own, do you?"

"No," I whispered. Pulling back from her, I stared

at her dim outline, dark against the dark. Why was I trusting her so much? Who was she, really?

"John," she said, "he didn't send me. I came because I wanted to. But *you* have to be sure, too." And she went as quietly as she had come, leaving me feeling more alone than I had ever felt before.

28

When I woke the next morning, light was pouring through the window, the dust specks churning slowly through the air like stars in a tiny, golden universe.

Curled over on one side, I lay very still, my eyes open, wondering yet again at all that had happened. Most of all I thought about the night before, when Ann had come to my room, what she had said, what I had thought and said.

Why, I asked myself, had I doubted myself, or let her know I had any doubts? She'd come to my room, and I, like a fool, had been . . . well, stupid.

Quickly, I slung on some clothes and opened the door. Not a sound. Moving softly, I went to her room and knocked on the door. No answer. I knocked again, but still got no reply. Puzzled, I edged the door open and looked in. She was gone.

I went downstairs. On the kitchen table I found a note explaining that she and Martin had gone to the hospital, that she would take Martin to his Scoutmaster's house and then come back home.

I decided to shower, got dressed, ate breakfast, then returned to the living room, not knowing what else to do but wait for Ann.

I hadn't sat there for very long when, in the back of my mind—I was almost afraid to think about it—I realized I was concerned about her. If John Proud could do all he had done, he could just as easily harm her, too.

I suddenly remembered what he had told me about her, that he had tried to use her, but that he couldn't. When she had gone to the cemetery that first time, she had been frightened. She had told me so herself. But she hadn't seen him.

Why? Why had John Proud chosen me? Was it what Uncle Dave had said, that I had evil in me? ... What was it in me? I kept asking myself, what was it in me!

The kitchen phone began to ring. I hurried to answer it. "Hello?"

"Is that you, John?" came a voice. It sounded familiar, but I couldn't place it.

"This is the Fentons' home," I said. "Can I help you?"

"It was you I wanted to speak to."

"Who is this?"

"I'm disappointed. I thought you'd know."

I knew then: John Proud.

"Now do you know?"

"Yes."

"Delighted you've come. Welcome."

I didn't know what to say.

"You don't have to worry about Nora and Tom. I know you didn't really want to hurt them. Just wanted them out of the way."

"That's not true."

"As for Ann . . ." He laughed. Then the phone went dead.

Slowly I put the phone down. Even as I did there was a slight squeal of car brakes from the front of the house. Quickly, I moved toward the door, expecting it would be Ann. But before I reached the door I was stopped by a knocking. Ann wouldn't have knocked.

I stopped right there, not sure which way to move.

The knocking came again. Instead of going to the door, I bolted up the steps and into the room where I had slept. From there I peered through the window. In the driveway was a state trooper's patrol car. I drew my head back quickly.

From below I heard more knocking.

I backed out of the room and stood at the top of the staircase, trying to decide what to do. I had done nothing wrong. But I couldn't go downstairs and open the door.

I went into another room and pushed the curtain aside a bit. The trooper had moved from the door and was standing on the walkway, just looking at the house. It was the same trooper who had stopped us the day before.

As I watched, he got back into his car, backed out, and drove away.

29

I heard Ann pull into the driveway about eleven. She came in carrying a large shopping bag.

"How're your folks?" was the first thing I asked.

"Fine, considering. Mom has this big bandage on

106

her head and a black eye you wouldn't believe. Dad has an arm in a sling. They said to say hello."

I followed her into the kitchen.

There she busied herself pulling out stuff from the bag—packaged goods, like instant rice and soups, dried fruit. Finally she stopped what she was doing and we looked at each other.

"Hello," she said, her eyes tentative, shy.

"Hello," I returned. "You okay?"

"Sort of. You?"

"Pretty good," I said. But then I stepped forward and kissed her. And we just held each other.

She turned about and went on with what she had been doing.

Right off, I told her about the strange phone call and about the state trooper.

She stood a little straighter, her back to me. "About the accident," she said. "They were just driving along when someone leaped into the road. Happened real fast. Dad reacted instinctively, trying to avoiding hitting him. Even at that, he said that he had this funny sense that it . . . was you on the road."

I shook my head.

"He didn't believe it. Said it must have been in his head because he was thinking about you."

"What did you say?"

"Nothing."

"Did he ask about the call?"

She paused. "You know, I don't lie to my parents," she said. "But I said I had stopped at a store and just lost track of time. He believed me."

She turned around. Her eyes were swimming in tears.

"I don't think you should go with me," I told her.

"Sure," she snapped, "I'll drive you up there, tell you where to get out, turn around, and wait patiently to hear from you again, right?"

"Maybe that would be better."

"And maybe it wouldn't," she said bitterly.

"Ann, I don't know what's going to happen when I meet up with him. I just don't know."

"What do you want to happen?"

"Want?" The word exasperated me. I didn't know what I wanted anymore.

"Yes, what do you want? Don't you think you better know that?"

"I . . . I have to get rid of him."

"Well, what I want is to help you," she said.

We spent the next hour getting ready. She had a checklist of all the necessary things, from waterproof matches to moleskin for foot blisters to sit pads to the right kinds of food. Around her neck she had a compass and the penny whistle.

I watched her as she filled the backpack, balancing everything just right, putting everything in the proper place. Each time she put something in, she checked it off her list.

I helped her roll up her tent, stuff the sleeping bags into their sacks. She got another pack—it was her mother's—which wasn't as big as hers, and used it for my load: the tent and the sleeping bags.

"Isn't it awfully warm for stuff like this?" I asked.

"It can turn cold in a shot. Better to have more. Always."

She put together hiking clothes for me, a combo from the rest of the family.

"How much food you bringing?"

"Two days'."

"Do your folks know where we're going?"

"I told them we were just camping for a couple of days. We should be getting back about the same time they do. No problem. In fact, I think they feel better that we're going to be out of the house." She smiled. "Small town."

By one o'clock we were ready. She had hiking boots on. I didn't, but then I wasn't carrying that heavy load. She tried her pack, insisting that she put it on herself. It seemed very heavy to me.

"How heavy?" I asked.

"Forty pounds."

When we were set and had loaded the car, we made ourselves a lunch.

I couldn't eat. "You'll be sorry if you don't," she warned. I did the best I could.

"Ready?" she asked, putting her hand on mine. We gave each other a hug and just stood there for a while hanging on to each other.

"Thank you," I said. She didn't answer. Instead, the next moment she gave me a full kiss.

"Just promise me one thing," she said.

"What?"

"I need to know what's happening. *Everything*. No matter what or how bad. I have to trust you. Do you understand?"

"Yes."

"Then let's go."

We gave each other one more hug and started for the door.

PART FOUR

30

We drove in silence, going slowly up into the wooded hills. The sky overhead was absolutely clear, while on all sides the dark-green forest pushed close. By the side an occasional sprig of Queen Anne's lace stood tall, while here and there glistening laurel leaves brushed heavily against the hot tar road.

"I would have thought lots of people came here in the summer," I said. We had seen only a few cars.

"It's midweek. Weekends can seem crowded. Lots of couples. Kids too, along with mom and dad."

I had a new thought: "That John Proud, he must have had a wife. What happened to her?"

She glanced at me sharply. "Don't you know?"

I shook my head.

"He killed her."

The road spun upward until we hit the crunching gravel of the trailhead parking lot. The area was completely empty.

We parked and pulled our stuff out, locking the car. I put on my backpack, she did the same. Then we attached water bottles to the straps.

I noticed that Ann fussed a lot with the buckles. I wondered if I was acting nervous too. "You okay?" I asked.

She looked up, took a deep breath. "I forgot to give you something," she said, backing up to me. "The top compartment of my pack. There's a zip-lock bag with a map. Take it out."

I did. "I need to show you what the area looks like," she said.

"Why? We'll be together, won't we?"

"Just in case we get separated, or . . . something."

"You're right," I admitted, and unfolded the map. It was covered with details of small lines.

Ann explained: "These red lines show you the rise and fall of the land. The tighter they are, the greater the rise. Green for forest. White is open area. This is Highway 443. County road 315. We're right between, see? State Game Lands Number 211. St. Anthony's Wilderness here. Fort Indiantown Gap Military Reservation here. Blue Mountain there."

I nodded, but what I was hearing was Ann's tension.

"Here's the boundary to the military. We'll keep far away from that. The old railway bed. The Appalachian Trail runs right here along the ridge of Stony Mountain, Rausch Creek, Rausch Gap. The Cemetery. Cold Spring. Devil's Race, and Stony Creek. We're here, moving there. Get it?" She looked up at me. I saw then that she was upset and was trying to hide it. "You keep the map," she said. "I know the area. Ready?"

"I think so," I said, trying to find some way to comfort her.

"Only think?"

"You said be honest."

She tried to smile. "Good try. I'll be fine soon as we start."

"Let's go then," I said, and took the lead.

We skirted the main gate and in moments we were marching steadily on the old railroad trail, the overhead trees shielding us from the sun's hottest rays. Our pace was steady, not too difficult. Despite my intentions, the farther we went, the more

I felt myself tightening up, thinking about what we were doing, where we were heading.

"Ann," I said after a while, "I have to know something."

"Go on."

It took a few moments. "When I met John Proud . . . he said he tried to use you."

She stopped short.

"Only he said he couldn't."

She was staring down the roadway, away from me. "Did he tell you that?"

"Yes. And you told me how strange, frightened you felt when you first went up there. Did you see him?"

Reluctantly—or so it seemed—she turned to face me. There was pain on her face. She shook her head. "It did frighten me," she said, "like I told you, but I didn't see anything."

"How come he couldn't use you?" I asked. "He did a number on Uncle Dave. For a while anyway. Now me. Why not you?"

She shook her head. "I don't know," she said softly.

"Okay," I said, feeling anger, "then why *me*?"

"I don't know that either," she said, sounding sad.

"Want to know what I think?" I said. "It's not that I look like him—I must *be* something like he is. Wrong, or bad or . . . evil."

"You're *not* like him," said Ann quickly. She was looking fiercely right into my face. "The more you allow yourself to think that way, the easier it's going to be for him. You have to fight, John, you have to."

"I'll try," I said, though I was not at all convinced. Something seemed wrong.

We started on again. But my question still hung in the air: Why me? Why not her? Was I bad and she . . . well, good?

31

As we walked, I began to recognize the sights I had seen the first time. The ruins. The place where Uncle Dave had gotten sick. Finally, after over an hour of trudging, I saw the stone bridge ahead.

"That's the turnoff, isn't it?" I said, coming to a halt.

"Yes." She stopped too.

"I say we go right to the cemetery."

"Okay," she said. I started to move, but she paused, reached out a hand to touch me, only to let it drop. "I'm right here with you," she said.

We reached the bridge, swung down the Appalachian Trail, and then took the right fork to the cemetery.

Silence greeted us. Dazzling spikes of silent white sunlight cut through the interlocking leaves above. Nothing stirred. Nothing seemed alive. The stone that marked the burial place of John Proud was, as it had been before, askew, the slant a mocking gesture that spoke a lie: He was dead, but still he lived.

"It's not real," I whispered.

Yet *something* was there, a coming, a presence. The air itself seemed to grow in weight, settling over me, my shoulders, my arms and legs and hands, pulling me down. There was no place to go but into the earth itself.

Then the idea came to me: It would be so good to lie inside the earth, wrapped about by cool ground. I closed my eyes. I wanted to sink. I wanted to.

"He's near," I said, my own voice far.

Ann put out a hand and gripped my arm. As I

116

felt his presence grow, her grip tightened until it hurt. I didn't want to be hurt. I wanted only to be left alone, to sink. Now her grip seemed to pull me up, bodily, out of the ground, back to my body, my breath, myself.

"Ouch!" I cried, and shoved her hand away.

My cry broke the spell. At once there was noise; the midsummer racket of cicadas filled the air. Tree leaves began to shift. Light softened. Birds darted. I felt sweat trickling down my back.

"What was it?" I asked, feeling very dizzy.

She shook her head. "It was like a dream," she said. "And you were being pulled away. Did you feel that?"

"Yes."

"Was it him?"

"I think so."

"Did you see him?"

"No. Did you?"

She shook her head. "I didn't want you to leave."

I let out a long breath, feeling very weak. I pulled the pack off my back and let it fall heavily to the ground. Then I sank down.

"Are you all right?" she asked.

The moment she asked I remembered. "Ann, do I look the way Uncle Dave looked?"

Alarm came to her eyes. "Yes," she said.

I held out my hand. "Get me out of here," I cried, my throat feeling increasingly constricted.

She helped me up. Quickly, I slung the backpack on. "Get me to the bridge," I said. "Don't let go of me."

Taking my hand, she held it tightly and moved fast, all but dragging me, constantly looking back at me.

In moments we reached the bridge. I threw off the pack and scrambled down to the swiftly flowing brook. Kneeling, I put my face into the water, running it up into my hair. It was shockingly cold.

I gulped and sat back up, shook my head the way a dog shakes a wet coat of fur. Ann, having left her pack above, was squatting by my side.

"I'm okay," I said.

Once back to the top of the bridge, I looked around for a place to rest. I was weary. There was a gravel pit a few yards off the roadway. I went there and stretched full out, using my pack as a pillow.

"Can you tell me what happened?" Ann asked as I lay there.

"He was trying to get me," I said. "That's his

place. It was like he would replace me right there. I can't do anything there. He's too powerful."

She listened.

"It has to be somewhere else," I said.

"Where?"

"I don't know," I said, closing my eyes. "Some-place." I thought hard. Then I remembered. "Where's that map?"

She pulled it out of my pack.

"Tell me some of those places again," I said. "By name."

She began to read them: "Rausch Gap. Rausch Village. Stony Mountain. Sharp Mountain . . ." She went on. But when she read, "Devil's Race," I said, "Stop! Devil's Race. What is that?"

She studied the map. "A fairly deep creek."

"Why's it called a race?"

"Look here," she said, showing me the place on the map. The lines were tightly packed. "You can tell—it's some sort of deep gorge. When it's full the water really races."

"Why Devil?"

"I don't know."

"Is it far?"

"About five miles."

"How long will it take to get there?"

119

"Two, two and a half hours." She studied the map. "The final part is off the Trail."

I looked at her. "What do you think?"

Again she considered the map. "It's not far from the military camp boundary."

"That doesn't matter, does it?"

"Long as we keep away. Why do you think that's a good place?"

"I don't know," I admitted. "It just sounds right." I took a swig from the water bottle she offered. "I have to find him, and it has to be some kind of neutral ground."

"Devil's Race doesn't sound neutral."

"Where else? Can we camp there?"

"I suppose."

"I want to go there," I said, and sat up.

"Rest another minute," she said. "I'll go refill the water bottles."

"Thanks."

She stayed a moment longer. "We could go home," she said.

"I don't want to."

She became thoughtful for a moment. "Be right back," she said, and went. I watched her go, thinking how lucky I was to be with her. Briefly, I closed my eyes. When I opened them, John Proud was sitting opposite me.

32

He was sitting on the ground, arms wrapped about drawn-up knees, a relaxed, easy smile on his face.

"Feeling better?" he said.

I gave a quick glance in the direction Ann had taken. I could no longer see her.

"Don't worry," he said. "She needn't know I've come at all, not unless you tell her. That's up to you."

I started to move. He held up a hand.

"Listen to me," he said, becoming more serious in manner. "You did well back there in the cemetery. You're just as smart as I hoped you'd be. If you had stayed much longer . . ." He didn't finish what he started to say.

"What would have happened?"

"Oh, what I told you would happen. The less you are, the more I become."

"What do you mean?"

"Oh, I know, you think I mean to murder you. But I promise—my word of honor—nothing like that at all."

"Then what?"

"I want to come back, John, to the world. It's that simple. But I can't, not like this." He made a gesture indicating himself. "I can frighten, alarm, but very little else. Really. In some cases, as with your Uncle Dave, that was enough. But I want to do more. To do more, I need to *be* more. So, you see, we need to replace one another." So saying, he reached out and tapped me on the hand.

The first time I had felt his touch—that time we shook hands in the cemetery—it was little more than a point of pressure, like the wind. Now, as he tapped me, I felt something more, a flickering sensation, as if I were touched by a hand.

"See?" he said, as if reading my thoughts. "Already I've gained. The more you struggle against me, the more I shall become, while you dwindle. In time . . . we will exchange places. Won't Ann be pleased? I intend to be bolder than you."

Summoning all my strength, I tried to hurl myself at him, moving forward as though ripping away ropes. But I passed right through him, no less than if he had been a cloud of smoke. I went sprawling beyond.

He laughed, then stood up. "Devil's Race," he said. "It isn't quite what I had in mind, but close enough. And you have Ann to lead you right there."

"Here's your water," said Ann's voice.

I spun about to find her there. Just as quickly I turned back to where John Proud had been. He was gone.

33

I started to say something, then stopped, realizing that Ann had seen nothing of him.

"What's the matter?" she asked.

I looked from her to the spot where John Proud had been.

"What *is* it?" she demanded.

I slumped back down, too confused and bewildered by what had happened.

"John," she repeated, "what is it?"

"And you have Ann to lead you right there," he had said. "It's okay," I said to Ann. "You startled me, that's all." I swung on my knees. She handed me the water bottle and I took my fill.

I capped it, then stood, aware that she was watching me, puzzled.

"Something happened, didn't it?" she asked. "No matter what, you have to trust me."

"I do," I said, but I was lying. I was sure there was something wrong, wrong about her, but I just couldn't figure it out.

"It's important," she said.

Again my doubts began to drift away. I lifted my hand and pressed the palm to the side of her face. She closed her eyes.

"Your hands," she said, "have such a very soft touch." She turned her face slightly and kissed my fingers.

I drew my hand back, trembling. Then I looked at her, too frightened to tell her my doubts.

We went westward on the Appalachian Trail, moving deep into the Wilderness. It was strange, beautiful country. We were walking through young forest, but, now and again, great bare mounds of black earth rose up. Under our feet, much of the earth was black too.

"Maybe a hundred or so years ago," Ann explained, "they used to mine coal here. The heaps are what they left. Then they went after the timber. You can see how thin the topsoil is. The area must have been totally devastated, like after a war. It's coming back, but I read somewhere it takes at least two hundred years. The whole Wilderness is nothing but an open wound. Do you know, when it rains, the ground bleeds black?"

I set the pace, steady, pushing, but not uncomfortable, though I needed to stop and take water more often than she. It was hot under the trees.

We went along for about an hour, moving upward at first, then on a long, level plain. We didn't see a soul. It was as if we were alone in the world.

I tried not to think about John Proud and what he had said. I felt as if I were in a period of grace, a brief moment before the final struggle. I didn't want to think at all.

I kept my eyes on the woods all about us, allowed myself to feel the weight on my back, my stride, the place. I wanted to become part of the peace that was there.

At about four o'clock the trail broadened into an open area. I could see rings of stone full of old campfire ashes. Right in the middle of this space was a mailbox, like the kind you see on rural roads.

"Yellow Spring Village," Ann announced, and she let her pack down. I did the same. She stretched out, head against the pack.

"Look in there," she suggested, indicating the mailbox.

125

Inside was a ruled notebook, the kind they use in elementary schools. It was full of messages, dated over a period of the last couple of months. "From Georgia to Maine," one read. "Trucking on!" "Boy Scout Troop 16," read another, followed by the scrawls of some fourteen kids. I searched for the last entry.

"Welcome to Yellow Springs," it read, and it was signed "John Proud." Added was today's date.

I stared at it, shocked by how similar the handwriting was to my own.

"Interesting?" Ann called out.

34

She was stretched out, her eyes closed. I could hardly stay still. I poked at the ground, scraping up bits of black stone and flinging them at the mailbox.

"How close to Devil's Race?"

"We've made good time."

"I'd like to get there."

"Half an hour. Maybe a little more."

I stood up and adjusted my pack. "Let's go," I said.

Still she lay there. "Don't you want to rest some more?"

"Ann, I want to get there."

She opened her eyes and sat up, looking at me. "You're very edgy," she said. When I didn't reply, she got herself up slowly, and in a few moments we were on our way again.

At first the trail continued easily, with only a few dips and rises. But then, abruptly, it started to go up. I found myself forced to lean into the incline. I would go about twenty feet and stop, feeling sweat drip down my face. I drank lots of water.

"Careful about how much water you take," Ann warned. "That creek might be dry."

I continued to stumble along in the lead till we reached the top. Ann was hot and flushed, and though she carried lots more weight than I did, she wasn't in such bad shape.

We had reached the turnoff. "No more trail," she announced. "Bushwhack time."

Using her compass and the map, she set our course. Then it was she who led the way through the woods, downward.

It was harder than going up. My pack kept throwing me off balance. My toes dug into my shoe tips and hurt. I kept feeling like I was about to fall. And it wasn't easy to push our way through the underbrush.

Then, unexpectedly, a deep ravine opened out in front of us. Below, water churned, chewed by rocks. To either side of the ravine the rock face had been shaped and sculptured into smooth forms.

"This is it," announced Ann. "Devil's Race."

35

The last time I put up a tent was when I threw a blanket over my folks' card table, crawled inside, and read *Superman* comic books by flashlight. What Ann set up seemed almost magical to me: a brilliant blue-and-white bubble, supported by slender golden rods. It seemed to spring out of the ground science-fiction style, pegged down and ready to move into within moments. Inside the air was clear, with a soft light that gave a sense of a world apart.

Ann passed in the gear, leaving only the food outside. That done, she suggested we sit by the water.

We scrambled down into the gorge—about twenty feet deep—and sat at the water's edge. There, the smooth rocks were flesh warm. Ann pulled off her boots and double socks, then plunged her feet into the water. I did the same. The shock was delicious.

"Like it?" she asked.

"Absolutely."

We sat there side by side, just drifting in an easy quiet, lulled by the sweet sound of water rushing past.

But as I sat there I began to think about Ann and what had been happening since I had come. I recalled her suggestion that her folks had been hurt because of me, not John Proud . . . or that I hadn't been honest to her . . . or that I didn't even know my own mind. . . .

My anger—for that was what I was suddenly feeling—continued to grow almost before I realized it was anger. Once again the same questions I had had before seemed to thrust themselves upon me: Why me? Why not her? Maybe she wasn't so good after all. Maybe she was part of him, the way Uncle Dave had been.

I began to wish that she wasn't there, feeling that in some way she was hindering what I had to do . . . that it would be better to be alone.

Only after I had these thoughts did I become aware

that *his* silence, his presence, had replaced the quiet, replaced the very air with his breath. He was there, for exactly how long I did not know.

Stiffly, I sat up.

"What is it?" Ann asked, now aware of my change in mood.

"Don't you feel him?"

She shook her head.

"He's near . . ." I whispered.

Ann pulled her feet from the water and stood over me, looking in all directions. I searched too, trying to find his whereabouts, wondering what he would do.

A small movement on the rock caught my attention. I looked down. At first I lost it. Then I saw: an ant, an ant no bigger than a quarter of an inch, and crimson red, darting here, there, about the rock, close to Ann's foot. Its brilliance transfixed me. Another moment passed. Then I realized what it was that I was seeing: *him.*

I watched, astonished, fascinated.

The ant kept shifting, pausing, as if seeking a place about Ann's foot. Delicate feelers stroked the air. Joints flexed. The next instant he climbed on Ann's foot, moved over her heel, scurried around her ankle, going toward her bare toes.

Irritated, Ann bent down to brush the ant away,

130

only to lose her balance. She began to fall, tried to right herself, failed, screamed.

The scream brought me back to my senses. I shot out a hand, attempting to keep her from falling. Held, she twisted about, now falling toward me, reaching out, holding on, only to collapse by my side on her knee with a cry of pain.

For a moment she just lay there, gasping for breath. I hovered over her, not letting her go. "You all right?" I whispered.

"My ankle," she said between gritted teeth. "My ankle." She managed to push herself about, revealing a knee bloody where it had hit the rock.

Then she leaned down and began to rub her ankle. With a sudden movement, she dropped her foot into the cold water, only to lean back, grimacing with pain. "Damn . . ." she said between intakes of breath. "Oh, damn, that hurts. . . ."

She shook her head, pulled her foot out of the water, held it up, wiggled it, plunged it back. There were tears on her face.

I scrambled up and squatted down behind her, allowing her to rest against me. She was breathing hard.

"The cold water keeps it from swelling," she managed to say.

"Just take it easy."

131

"So stupid," she whispered. "Some bug on me. Did you see what it was?"

Feeling alarm, I just shook my head.

"I'm not going to be much help to you now," she said. "I won't be able to walk for a while."

"Ann . . ." I began, trying to find the courage to tell her what happened.

She closed her eyes and rested.

I looked about. A spot of color caught my eye. On the ground, not far away, was the red ant. It had stopped moving, as if waiting for me to act. I lifted my hand to strike when I realized that he had only done what I had been thinking about, found a way to leave Ann behind.

In a rage I brought my hand down. But he had fled.

36

Ann stirred. "Just a sprain," she said. "But this is nice." She snuggled back against me.

I felt worthless.

"It'll take a while to ease up," she added. "We'll

have to stay put. Me, anyway." She moved so she was leaning against my chest. "Put your arms around me," she said.

I did, mechanically.

"It's lovely here," she said. Her head dropped back, resting on my shoulder. Her eyes were closed. She wrapped her arms around mine, hugged them. "Lord, it hurts, and that water is freezing."

I felt my own tension rising again.

Turning slightly, she tilted her face toward mine, kissing the side of my mouth.

"And you have Ann to lead you right there." John Proud's words.

She's acting as if nothing has happened, I told myself.

Then I began to think back. Only when I was with her, I suddenly realized, did *he* appear. Was that true? She was close when I first saw him. And she was the one who led me, *twice*, to the cemetery. Wasn't she the one who told me, by phone, all the things he had done? How did I know about them, except that *she* told me? I had believed everything she said. Just that day when I asked her why John Proud hadn't used her, how pained she had looked. But she hadn't really given an answer.

"And you have Ann to lead you right there."

133

In my mind I heard Uncle Dave's words: *"If all you have are questions, you haven't listened to the answers."*

I had an answer now.

She was part of him. She was using me, for him.

"What is it?" she said. "What are you thinking about? You look awful. What's the matter?"

Too stunned to speak, I just shook my head.

She shifted her body away, drew her foot out of the water, wiggled, and looked at it. Without looking at me, she said, "Please tell me. . . ." Her voice had become tired.

I pulled my legs around and stood up, trying frantically to decide what to do. She had brought me out there, into the Wilderness, and now she would no longer help me. That was their plan. I was completely alone.

"Are you going to tell me or not?"

"No."

"Why?"

I just shook my head.

After a moment she said, "I think I'll lie down in the tent. Give me a hand."

Not knowing what else to do, I reached out. Slowly, carefully, she drew herself up.

As we went, she hopping, me walking, she put

more and more weight on me, until at the front of the tent she eased herself down. There she sat, rubbing her ankle.

"Glad I brought along an Ace bandage," she said. "You never know what's going to happen."

I stood there, watching her, hating myself for what I had discovered, hating her too.

She looked up, suddenly alarmed. "Why are you looking at me that way?"

"You said you'd be honest," I blurted out.

"John, I—"

"Honest!" I suddenly shouted.

Startled, she drew back, confused. "I don't know what you're talking about."

"You're with him, aren't you? You are!"

Again she shook her head. "John—"

"I didn't make all those things happen. Not one of them. Only you made me think it was me. I didn't. I never did. I had nothing to do with any of it. It was him, and you! But it's me he's trying to destroy, not you. Well, I wish it was you! I do!" Unable to look at her, I turned, full of tears.

"None of that is true," I heard her say. "None of it."

I said nothing.

Then she said, "I'm going to lie down for a while."

Her voice was soft, sad. It was all an act. I didn't believe her and I didn't care what happened to her either.

She crawled into the tent.

I stood outside, alone.

37

Faintly, the thumping of the guns. At first they were distant, as they always had been. But as the barrage continued, it grew louder. Vaguely, I remembered we were much closer to the military area.

Anger had taken me over. I had been tricked, humiliated, turned into a fool. Wanting nothing more than just to go away, I went back down by the creek, into Devil's Race. There I watched the water, watching its surface constantly fold in upon itself, back, down, and around.

How long I sat there I don't know. It might have been minutes. It might have been hours. When I looked up it had grown darker. Thin gray filled the air. The stillness smothered me. I felt like an empty shell, hollow at the core. I was cut off, isolated even from myself, lost in my own wilderness.

* * *

He had returned.

He appeared quite suddenly, a few feet from where I was sitting. I looked at him.

"Well, now," he said, "we've come a decent way, haven't we? You seem to be very much a wiser young man." He gave his smile.

"Let me show you how far we have progressed," he said. "You are sitting on rock, aren't you? Now then, take your hand and lay it, palm down, flat against it. Go on. Do it."

Reluctantly, I did as he told me.

"Now push, *push.*"

I looked at him, at my hand . . . and then . . . I pushed. To my astonishment my hand sank into the rock until I could no longer see my fingers or my wrist.

He laughed.

"Wiggle your fingers. Go on. You can do it."

I did.

"What do you feel?"

What I felt was an even, unyielding pressure, as if my hand was encased in a strong, but somewhat gentle, cool mass.

"You are feeling the inside of a stone," he said. "Like death, in fact. Not so bad, is it?"

I attempted to snatch my hand out. For a moment

it held. I felt terrified. Then I broke free and held my hand before my face.

"All there," he said. "But you see, the more I am, the less you are. Just as I promised. Death isn't so very bad, John. Peaceful. No one can bother you. Think of it." He stood up.

I did the same.

"Why don't you just give up, John? You would like to."

All I wanted was to get away from him. I slid down the gorge, plunged through the water and across.

"Trying to lose me?" he called.

I sprang to the other side, taking the incline. Repeatedly slipping, I had to scramble on all fours, grabbing rocks and shrubs. I reached the top and looked back where I had come from. He had vanished. Only the blue dome of the tent stood like some window to another world behind me.

I looked about, searching the dark woods for some way to escape. I no longer cared about anything. I wanted nothing to do with anyone.

I wanted to give up.

Turning from him and from Ann, I walked into the woods. I heard his laughter. I kept on going. There was nothing I did not hate, myself most of all.

38

I wandered with no trail, no particular direction. St. Anthony's Wilderness. I might have been on the moon for all the life I saw. Wherever I moved the silence, his silence, seemed to hover. Whatever lived there—animals, birds—hid, waiting for me to pass so they could live again. I was being shunned.

I did not care what happened to me.

I came to an old tree, its roots exposed and bent above the earth. The area overlooked something of a hollow, at the bottom of which lay decaying rubbish. I sat down, leaned against the tree, and closed my eyes. I was so very tired.

I tried to think over what had happened, holding my greatest anger for Ann. Once again I saw how she had used me, tricked me. And now, in her way, by abandoning me, she was about to destroy me.

The more I thought about her, the less I thought about John Proud. The idea that I had liked her so much, wanted to make love to her, was awful to me. I supposed I had loved her.

139

At some distance the guns beat. The pounding, slow and methodical, seemed to be at one with my heart.

A piece of rotten wood lay on the ground. I picked it up. White bugs that had clung to it scurried away. I poked the damp bit with my finger, pushing it through. But when I removed my finger there was no hole.

"Maybe," I thought, "Ann is dead."

"Maybe," I thought, "I am."

Nothing mattered.

The silence around me became suffocating. I gagged for breath. John Proud. I didn't care about him either.

I cared about nothing. Not even myself.

I stood up, trying to decide which way to go. I started to walk back in the direction I thought I had come from. Sure enough, as I went on, I found evidence that I was going the right way. A footprint here, there, matching mine. A broken twig now and again suggested I was moving correctly.

I was proud of myself. I wasn't lost. I didn't need anyone to show me the way. I knew exactly where I was going. I was in charge.

Out of nowhere came his laugh.

I saw then. It was too easy what I was doing, simply following signs in the woods. Too many signs. Had I made them? Or had he?

I felt my skin prickle. . . .

That day, that day when I had first come to the Wilderness, I had been glad that Tom Fenton had not been able to come. I had wanted him to be called elsewhere. I had wanted Ann to come. And I had wanted Uncle Dave out of the way.

Other thoughts began to pour in on me. I began to think of all the things I had wanted. I had wanted to get rid of Ann.

I! I!

My heart was racing.

Everything I had wanted had been done for me.

"All that happens will be your doing. Your wanting. Don't ever forget that, ever!"

John Proud had said that the first time.

So all those things that had happened, *all* of them, were things that had let me do what *I* wanted. . . . I, myself.

But if that was so, why had I wanted to hurt Ann, to leave her? . . . Because I did not want her to know that truth—that evil—in me.

141

For another moment I stood there. I saw then that John Proud had not fooled me. He had only shown me a way to fool myself.

I began to run, leaping, crashing through the underbrush, back to where I had left Ann.

I hit the top of the gorge—Devil's Race—almost at a full gallop. I hurled myself down through the water, up to the other side and the tent.

There I stopped, afraid to look.

I dropped to all fours, went to the tent, and threw back the entrance flap. Ann was there, lying absolutely still.

"Ann?" I called softly. "Ann . . ."

She gave no answer.

Frantic, I scrambled inside. "Ann," I called again. Shaking, I put out my hand, let my fingers touch her lips. I could feel nothing.

And I, I had done it, done it all, every bit. I, John Proud.

In a daze I backed out of the tent. And he was there, directly opposite, on the other side of the ravine.

"Yes, you did that too," he called, "and she trusted you, John. Well, surely now you know I've all but won. It's time to finish, isn't it?" And he turned and began to run away in long, easy strides.

That time *I* ran after *him*.

That time I would not give up.

39

I ran blindly, falling as I ran, down the steep hills, following where he had gone. It was an area thickly set with boulders and broken trees, the trees like bowling pins knocked this way and that. I careened from point to point, my eyes trying not to lose him.

From time to time I did. Never for long. He seemed always just beyond, just out of reach, with an ease that only made me angrier.

"Here," he would call, taunting me. "Here!"

And I followed.

We kept moving down. The murky light of the long dusk made false shadows. Then I would break into a small clearing, and again it would be day. I was running through time.

I had no idea what I would do when I caught him. More than once I was certain I never would. Worse, I felt like I was chasing myself. He not only looked like me, he seemed to be able to read my mind, to *be* my mind. I would think of going one way to cut him off. He would appear to fall into the trap, but then at the last moment he would break free.

I broke out onto a dirt road that cut at right angles to the way he was going. I stood there, trying to get my breath back, wondering which way he had gone. For the moment I lost him.

I waited, sure he would show himself. And he did, below, beyond the road. I took a deep breath, and raced after.

Soon I came to a small creek. I skipped across and once more the land shifted. Now I was laboring up. More and more it seemed to me that he had some particular place in mind. On all fours, crawling much of the time, I pressed on, catching glimpses of him above.

I reached the topmost ridge, and another dirt road. But on the far side was a steel mesh fence, seven feet high. On top, tipped forward, barbed wire. It extended to either side as far as I could see along the fence.

Beyond this fence was an open area of some forty feet, and then another fence, equally high, also topped with barbed wire.

I looked up and down and saw no way to get through. I wasn't sure if John Proud had. After walking up and down a bit, I noticed that on the inner fence was a sign:

**WARNING! KEEP OUT! DANGER!
U.S. MILITARY RESERVATION!!!**

He was nowhere in sight. Spent, I leaned against the fence, trying to make up my mind which way to go. And there he was against the second barrier, leaning too and looking right at me!

Casually, as if he had nothing to fear from me, he turned and began to move away. In my frustration I gripped the metal hard. To my astonishment, my fingers slid through the wire. I thrust my hands forward and my arms too. They went through. I stood there, awed, looking at my hands on the other side of the fence.

With a sudden, impulsive push, I flung myself at the fence and . . . went through to the other side.

Horrified yet elated, I stood there, trembling. Then I raced for the second fence, and without flinching tore through it.

Catching a glimpse of him below, I dove after him, redoubling my speed, crashing down to the bottom and onto a field. There I stopped and looked about to see where it was I had come.

The field was horribly mangled, with nothing but splintered stumps of trees, some charred, some smoldering. Even the ground felt warm. Gaping holes in the ground seemed to have been scooped out by giant hands. I made my way around them.

I stood, listening, for I had again lost sight of him. The deep silence told me he was close, very close. Then I heard something new. It was a high, shivering, whispering whistle. I could not place it. Then I saw it, a black stroke against the sky. The next instant, some thirty yards in front of me, the earth erupted, a fountain of dirt and rock. At almost the same time there came a roar. Wind hurled upon me, threw me down in a rain of earth.

I pushed myself up on my hands and knees, wiping the dirt from my face. I heard a distant thud. Then again the whipping, whishing sound, followed in seconds by a crash, as elsewhere in the field, that time *behind* me, the earth shook, leaped and rained.

He had led me into the cannon target zone.

40

I felt tears running down my face, the bursting emptiness inside, my own voice telling me that I deserved to die, that this was fair punishment for all that I had done.

"I'm here!" I screamed. "I'm here!"

Only that ghastly roar gave reply, and the shaking of the earth. And through it all, like strokes of a whip, the high, whispering whine of the shells as they slit the air.

Then I saw him—John Proud—standing in the middle of the field as if he were at the beach taking his ease. He was watching me, watching what happened to me, waiting for me to die so he could take my place.

I hated him. I wanted to destroy him.

Slowly, carefully, focusing on him, I began to move. He had made me all but nothing. The cannon could not hurt me. Pain would have been relief, some proof that some of me was left. I was beyond pain.

I drew closer.

He held his place, waiting.

I picked up a rock, a large one, and hefted it in both hands.

He stood there waiting, patiently waiting.

I came within a few feet of him. He had not so much as moved or flinched. Lifting the stone, feeling its great weight, I hurled it with all my strength right at him.

It struck with a crash.

To my amazement he shattered, shattered like so many bits of glass. A mirror.

For a second my heart leaped at the thought that I *had* destroyed him. But even as I felt that joy he was there again, exactly as before, the image of myself, only stronger, clearer.

"You must kill me," he taunted, "with your own hands. That's the only way. I *want* you to!"

I stood there, my hands up, ready to do his bidding. He waited. He wanted me to kill him. He wanted me to act.

But standing there I began to understand something: He was my mirror, but then I must be his. If I destroyed him, that very act would make me him. *That* was what he wanted. My hatred would match his. And he would then be able to take my place. That would be his ultimate victory, his triumph.

So I stood there, staring at his face that was my face, watching myself, hating myself. I no longer knew who he was. Had he become me? Or I him? Had we already switched?

Questions . . . answers . . .

148

"Kill me," I heard a voice say. "It's what you want."

I did not even know who was speaking.

Were we one, or two . . . or both . . . ?

"Hate me!" he screamed. "Hate me!"

And then . . . I did know. It was not a question. It was not an answer. "Were we one, or two?" The question was the answer.

They were not separate. They were one. As we were. Inseparable.

And I knew then the only way to save myself.

Instantly, I leaped upon him. But instead of trying to kill him, I embraced him.

Taken by surprise, he struggled to get free. I would not let him go.

As the earth exploded all around us, I clung to him with a desperation and pain I had never known. All I knew was that I must not let him go. I must hold him, accept him.

In the middle of that field of fire, locked together, he now in terror, as I was, we were equal—good, bad—two parts of one come together at last. And I screamed with all the voice I ever had, "We are one!"

There was a gigantic explosion.

I was lifted, turned, spun through the air, high,

higher, on a spiral, until I landed with what felt like the weight of all matter over me, deep, deep, within the dark of my own heart.

It was as if I had entered into the middle of a stone.

41

I woke slowly. My mind was floating free in some place, some time. "Am I dead or alive?" I asked myself.

I opened my eyes to blackness.

Gradually I saw the flickering of light. Starlight.

Painfully, I pushed myself up. Dirt fell from my body.

The pale light of the moon filled the broken field with a gentle, yellow-rose glow.

I heard night sounds.

Working hard, I managed to stand up. Not sure which way to go, I looked about in a wide circle. In one direction was high ground. That would be, I knew, St. Anthony's Wilderness. I went that way.

I reached the first fence. Remembering how I had come through before, I held up my hands and attempted to push through the wire. My hand sprang back. I could no longer get through that way.

I walked along the fence in search of some way to get through. A hole perhaps.

I found a tree that had fallen against the fence, tearing down the topmost barbed wire. I shimmied up and dropped over.

The second fence was harder. No trees. No holes. But, increasingly impatient, I climbed it with only a few scratches.

I walked across the road, then down from the ridge. Once more I began to climb. Now I was in the forest, in the absolute dark. I no longer knew which way to go.

My thoughts returned to Ann. Grief filled me. I had betrayed her.

I began to cry then, the tears slipping down my face. I was crying not just for myself but for her, what she was, what I had destroyed. I had loved her. I wished that she was there with me, that she loved me. What was I to do with what I had done?

I wanted her to be alive.

And then I heard it.

It was faint at first, but unmistakable. It came to me like a thin bright thread of hope, gliding through the trees, the clear, simple tune of her penny whistle.

It was beautiful. And it sang to me, called me, led me.

42

I came out on the far side of Devil's Race, directly opposite the tent. Ann was sitting there, her legs crossed, her feet bare, her ankle still wrapped in the bandage.

"Ann!" I called.

The music stopped. She looked up and smiled. "I thought," she said, "that if I played long enough you would find your way."

We crawled into the tent and lay down side by side.

She put her arms around me, pressed her face close to mine.

"I love you," I said.

"I love you too."

We held each other.

And I knew that I was there, all of me at last, whole and free.